W9-AHS-424

More Praise for Brian Keith Jackson's
THE VIEW FROM HERE

"An excellent first novel . . ."
—*The Oakland Press* (CA)

"Read with wonder and gratitude this tender, wise novel of women's lives and welcome a fresh new voice to the company of storytellers like Kaye Gibbons."
—Sandra Scofield, author of *A Chance to See Egypt*

"Well-written . . . compelling . . . Jackson presents a female point of view with a commitment and sympathy almost totally nonexistent in novels by black men."
—James Coleman, *The News & Observer* (Raleigh, NC)

"Ladies and gentlemen, meet Brian Keith Jackson. He's seen what you've seen and heard what you've heard, but he has the eye and ear of a true storyteller, and a storyteller's ability to tell the old tales with fresh words and fresh insight."
—Dale Peck, author of *The Law of Enclosures* and *Martin and John*

"A beautiful story of love, family, and a friendship so strong that its bonds continue despite a great distance. . . . The creativity of this author is certainly refreshing. Jackson has a wonderful gift for storytelling in which he incorporates humor, compassion, understanding, and an interesting cast of characters."
—Susan Pashley, *The Pilot* (South Pines, NC)

"Touching . . . In Anna, Jackson has created a memorable and genuine heroine."
—Merle Rubin, *The Christian Science Monitor*

"An assured fiction debut . . . Jackson's ready powers of storytelling will win over readers."
—*Out* magazine

"A writer to watch in the future . . . Jackson provides a tender understanding of a woman's struggles as she is surrounded by men and an unfeeling sister-in-law. . . . Jackson leaves readers guessing until the last few pages as to how Anna's pregnancy will end."
—Christi Gifford, *Orlando Sentinel* (FL)

"If there is any debate about the potential of the young literary lions coming on the scene, that will be eliminated by the arrival of Brian Keith Jackson's *THE VIEW FROM HERE*. . . . Jackson has a sure feel for dialogue and a sumptuous sense of time and place."
—*BookPage*

"Jackson's debut novel should not fly, but it does—and wonderfully so. . . . Jackson forces readers to the edge of their seats . . . in this wisdom-soaked, beautifully told tale."
—Beth E. Andersen, *Library Journal*

The View From Here

BRIAN KEITH JACKSON

WASHINGTON SQUARE PRESS
PUBLISHED BY POCKET BOOKS

New York   London   Toronto   Sydney   Tokyo   Singapore

An excerpt from *The View from Here* first appeared in *Shade: An Anthology of Fiction by Gay Men of African Descent*, published by Avon Books in June 1996.

A Washington Square Press Publication of
POCKET BOOKS, a division of Simon & Schuster Inc.
1230 Avenue of the Americas, New York, NY 10020

ISBN: 0-671-56896-5

First Washington Square Press trade paperback printing February 1998

10 9 8 7 6 5 4 3 2 1

WASHINGTON SQUARE PRESS and colophon are registered trademarks of Simon & Schuster Inc.

Cover design by Jeanne M. Lee
Cover photos: woman © Lloyd Wolf/Swanstock; clouds © Bettmann Archive; field © Impact Visuals/Jerome Friar/PNI

Printed in the U.S.A.

For my parents,
as well as those here, gone and
forthcoming

Acknowledgments

To whom so much of this belongs:

Charlotte Abbott; Eraka Bath; Phillip Christian; my editor, Dona Chernoff, and the entire Pocket staff; Paul Edward Hayes Cooper; Dr. William L. Goldberg; Cheryl Hulteen; Brandon Keith Jackson; Lloyd Stafford Jolibois, Jr.; Christopher Kelly; Kristin Lang; Dr. Adrian C. Lawrence; Douglas Levere; Bruce Morrow; David Paul; Jeffrey Howard Pennington; Monti Sharp; Sandra Scofield; my agent, Emma Sweeney; Jacqueline Woodson; and Diane Vuletich.

Art Matters, Inc., the Big Cup, Jacqui, Jay, and the Grange Hall, Gant and Ian of Salon Wednesdays, Teachers & Writers Collaborative, my entire family, and the numerous others that have made this more than just a possibility.

Twinkle, twinkle, little star . . .

1

Dear Ida Mae:

I have a moment, so I had to make myself cherish the stillness, as it doesn't come easily these days. Not a day goes by that I don't look out in the distance, hoping, wishing I'd see a vision of you coming my way. Many of those days, I truly believe I see you, the sway of your dress and that glow about you. But as my heart starts to dance, I know that it's just my mind playing a lonely tune, leaving me blinded by what I can't see. So, yes, I write to fill the stillness. I have so many letters to you but no way of sending them. The mailman is a constant reminder of that. Still, I hold on to them, sure that one day, I'll be able to pass them on to you. For now, they serve as much out of need as desire . . .

I'm pleased to say I'm expecting another baby. You're the first person I've told, and it feels good to say it—if not out loud, then on paper. I've been looking for the right time to tell Joseph. I fear there is no such thing as the right time. All the same, this baby is growing inside me. This one is a girl, Ida Mae. I just know it. I know it sounds crazy, but I can feel the difference.

Momma's not here to tell me, but some things you just know . . . .

"White folks always love li'l colored babies," says my momma to my poppa when she decided to tell him she was carrying me. "Miss Janie won't mind if I bring her to work with me. She loves colored chilren. She's always sayin' how clean and well behaved colored chilren are. 'None more mannered than a colored child,' she says. It won't be no problem. No problem at all. You remember how she was with Junior, when he was coming up? Sweet as she could be. Treated him just as good as if he was one of her own. Remember? She would give us old books and toys that her chilren had outgrown. Remember?"

Momma was saying all this to convince herself. She had this conversation, with the walls that framed our house, on many occasions, until the words were placed as neatly as the seams of the paper that covered them. But all that seemed fruitless now. She knew Poppa was trying not to hear her conversation. She had been putting off telling him for as long as she could, constantly reminding herself of his saying he didn't want "no mo' chilren"; it had been seven years since Momma was last pregnant. She had an idea as to how Poppa was likely to take the news of me, but through it all, remained hopeful. He had said time and time again that he already had "too many mouths to feed." I would make number six.

Momma was well into her fifth month with me and hiding it was no longer possible. The winter months, if you want to call them that, though never severe, were over, stripping her of her deceiving layers. She could no longer blame it on putting on a few pounds here and there to fight off the cold that, to hear everyone talk, was always "goin' 'round." She was showing and there was nothing else to do but to tell Poppa, hope, and pray for the best.

"It's not going to be no trouble, J. T." My momma always calls Poppa J. T. when she's trying to get on his good side. It makes things seem more personal-like. Poppa's full name is Joseph Henry Thomas. People who know him, including those that work at the lumber mill, just call him Joe.

"I can get baby clothes from Miss Janie, bein' her two chilren grown now, J. T. She wouldn't a bit mind me usin' the clothes she's got stored away up in her attic. They're just sittin' up there in boxes collectin' cobwebs. The only thing cobwebs are good for are spiders. She's got no use for those clothes now. I'm almost sure she wouldn't mind. J. T.? Well, anyhows, I'll talk to her when I go to work on Monday. How's that sound? J. T.?"

Poppa didn't say a word. He just kept eating, adding more to the place that held his answer before what was already there could be swallowed.

Momma had been in the kitchen all day preparing his favorites—catfish, collard greens and fatback, hotwater bread, and the purple hull peas she had bought from the farmers' market a whiles back and thawed out today to cook just for this occasion. For dessert, blackberry cobbler with sugar sprinkled on top of the crust, "just like you like it, J. T."

Momma had been antsy and riled. She cooked and talked to me, saying not to worry, everything was going to be all right and Poppa would come around. It would just take some doing and that I'd see. I'd see, everything was going to be just fine.

She had to sit down every now and again. The heat from the stove would make her dizzy. Mississippi's springs may be filled with rain, but when it isn't raining, the temperature is never anything to play with lightly. Many a day you can see the heat dancing in the distance, blurring the view.

After Poppa ate, she filled his Mason jar with iced tea and three wedges of lemons, "just like you like it, J. T.," and he went out on the porch to read the *Free Press,* the colored newspaper. Poppa never drank a drop with the meal—always after, to wash his food down. Though the sun had made a night of it, it was still hot and humid out, and the jar began to sweat, each drop finding its way to the next, making a clean but crooked trail down to the wooden planks, where it left a ring, joining stains from years past.

He sat in his rocker. It was his rocker and no one dared sit in it or even joke about doing so. It was like he could tell if someone else's behind had been there. He once said he knew if someone had been in his chair because of an "ol' war injury." Momma said Poppa was just poking fun, that he'd never been in no war—no war to speak of. Even if company came over, which was rare, Momma would offer her chair, never his. It was his property to do with as he pleased—as was Momma and, for the time being, as was I.

"How was your meal, J. T.? Ever'thing sit right with you? I made it special for you. Spent the whole day. Me and the baby," says Momma, coming out on the porch. "Was work all right? I heard tell that things are pickin' up all over and people are orderin' more. Sounds like good news. Doesn't it?"

Poppa remained silent. His huge hands gripped the *Free Press* at each side. He had the kind of hands that were like iron, more like what you would expect to see on a statue in the town square instead of on a living, breathing man. The wedding band on his third finger seemed small compared to the knuckle that many years of labor had built up. Poppa's been working at the mill lifting and moving lumber for the last twenty-some-odd years. His body is naturally built by a day-to-day routine that the trees of nature control.

Momma kept on talking, her voice filled with promise. Poppa never flinched. He just continued staring at the paper, or at least looking at the pictures that centered each page. Momma began to cry. She knew not to do so too loudly or in his presence, but all the same the tears fell, silently, as tears so often do.

She went back into the house and sat near the door to watch his every move. The mean meantime sat with her. My brothers knew when my father was this way they'd best just sit down and be as quiet as possible, whereabouts they don't cause any distractions. Even the slightest squeak from the pine floors could prove to be the lightning that set off a clap of thunder. As I said, Poppa was heavy-handed, and no one wanted to get in the way of those hands. Through experience, they knew any li'l thing could set him off. Today, I was that li'l thing.

Momma kept sitting, watching him. She was watching him so close I could feel her breaths become his. Breathing out, then in, as he did, three becoming one. His lungs seemed to be the keyhole to the future, entrance to the other side.

"You can have the chile," says Poppa, not even

looking away from the paper, as if the words were written on that very page and he was just reading them.

Momma's breaths became her own, ours, again as she swung open the screen door, running out to his side. "Thank you, J. T. Thank you."

"But you cain't keep it. We cain't risk it. It might be two again. My back is breakin' awready and I don't need another screamin' chile runnin' 'round keepin' up racket. Clariece cain't have no chilren and she need some help 'round they place. If they be willin', we'll give it to them to raise so James's name can go on. I'll go 'round pay a visit on Sunday. Talk to 'em 'bout it."

After that, Poppa said no more. He had spoken, and nothing more need be said. Momma knew this. There was no need to question something that had been settled. As fast as swatting away an anxious fly, happiness fell from her face to the splintering planks on the porch floor, where the rings of water awaited company.

Taking the same steps as she did moments before, she walked back through the screen door, careful to catch it before it slammed, not wanting to disturb Poppa and make matters worse. It was hard to believe things could get much worse, but Momma didn't want to chance it. Many thoughts ran through her head, never forming a complete picture. Thinking became a thing of the past. Reality had canceled what was, at least until this day, a possibility waiting to spring forth.

For five months, she had waited for the words to come out of her mouth, waited for an answer. Now, she had one.

Clariece is Poppa's older sister. She's the only living kin he has left. She married James, a preacher, some time ago but wasn't able to provide a living child. Three had made their way through her, but all had died before they ever took their first gasp. It didn't seem as if Clariece'd be able to provide James with a name child.

After washing up the supper dishes on Saturday evening, Momma pulled out the ten-pound iron, putting it on the stove. After testing it with a spit-moistened finger, she took out the ironing board and pressed everybody's Sunday clothes. Everybody's but Poppa's. Poppa never went to church. Didn't believe in it. But he always made my brothers go to represent the family. He didn't want Momma going by herself. The eyes of the Lord may have been good enough for everyone else, but he wanted only his eyes peering down on Momma.

Since Poppa had made his decision as to what would become of me, Momma had been dreading this evening. She knew the day after—Sunday, tomorrow—would determine my fate. Poppa would talk to James and all would be decided—decided without her voice, a voice that only I can seem to hear.

After she pressed the clothes, she hung them up so in the morning my brothers could get ready without too much of a fuss. Any kind of uproar tomorrow would easily prove to be too much for her, for us.

Momma and I were always the last ones to bed. It was our quiet time. If Poppa and his friends were out at the Rusty Nail, the local juke joint, we would always wait up just in case somebody wanted something to eat, making sure the liquor would have something to stick to in the night, relieving a foggy head from entering a new, clear morning.

"Now, I know you're worried, but ever'thing's goin' to be just fine," says Momma, rubbing her stomach and nibbling on the shiny top of the last piece of corn bread from tonight's supper. "We've still got time on our side. Time and the Lord. Between the two, you've got nothin' to worry about."

"Who you talkin' to?" says Poppa, opening the screen door. His voice silenced the crickets that always filled the night's air with a song of sufferance, pounding on the ear.

"J. T., I didn't hear you come up. How long you been standing there?"

"Long 'nough. I heard you talkin'. Who you talkin' to? I don't see nobody here. You talkin' to yaself? Only crazy folk talk to theyself."

"No, Joe. I'm just passing the time with li'l Lisa till you come home."

"Don't be callin' that chile no names. That ain't yourn to be doin'. That's for James and Clariece to do. Bad luck to be callin' it a bitch name anyhows. James don't need no more womens 'round, that's for sure. So don't be jinxin' this here baby. You hear? You hear?!"

"Yes, Joe. I hear you. No need in makin' no ruckus; you'll wake the boys."

"They mine to wake, ain't they?"

Momma doesn't answer, but with a smile she asks, "You want me to warm you up somethin', J. T.?"

"Nah. I'm goin' to bed. I gots to get up fo' day. It's gonna take a good spell to get over to James's place. I'll have to try and hitch a ride."

Poppa went on to bed. Momma and I stayed up a while longer, cleaning an already dust-free kitchen. Sometimes a clean spot can appear dirty if you stare at it long enough. Momma kept walking around on light feet, looking for old things, seen for the first time. Anything to pass the time, only to reach what would seem like forever. There wasn't any use in trying to sleep—not tonight.

Lisa. That's my name. "Li'l Lisa." I've been called that since the first day of sickness. Some folks may have thought it was a cold or that she had eaten something spoilt that made Momma sick. Never would they have conjured up the notion of a child.

Not now. Not after all these years. Maybe had there been other women around, they would have known. But Momma was the only one; after five children, you don't need no doctor or midwife to tell you you're expecting.

"Your Poppa doesn't mean no harm. I know at times it may sound like it, but he doesn't mean no harm." Momma says this to me without opening her mouth, fearing Poppa might overhear, waking a concern that, for the time being, needed to sleep. That was the kind of relationship we had. Momma and me. Momma wasn't so much afraid of Poppa, but she knew him better than he knew himself, and sometimes in that came the hurt, the understanding.

After sitting at that old wooden kitchen table until there was absolutely nothing else to do, Momma lowered the oil lamp. With held breath, we went and slid in bed beside Poppa. The cool sheets pacified us, embracing a body woed by the warmth of the day.

Just as we were getting comfortable and about to relax into rest, Poppa rolled over toward her. Placing his hand on Momma's shoulder, he rolled her from her side onto her back. The night wasn't over for us. Not just yet.

From what I'm told and what I've heard, Poppa wasn't always this way; he was kind and charming. I'm sure it's true, because Momma told me so.

Momma and Poppa met many moons ago at the Mt. Olive Church picnic when they were just "younguns." Of course, Poppa wasn't a member of the congregation, but he would show up for the social functions. Even the finest Christian wouldn't be evil enough to kick someone out of a church function. Besides, young boys could always get away with such devilment and it would be tolerated, even attractive. Boys will be boys, and girls will giggle at them, with muted mouth.

The place for all this socializing was always at a church function. All the best courting took place at these functions because this was where all the young people knew all the other young people would be, whereabouts they could see one another without sneaking around at night, risking getting a couple of rounds of buckshot sent their way for trespassing on somebody's property.

These functions were a guarantee that clothes would be pressed and baskets filled with the results of the best recipes each kitchen had to offer, each aiming to out-taste the rest. Young folks didn't have much opportunity to meet in social places with the other sex, so these picnics were the place, where, in the name of God, sinning was permitted.

I was told that first day, the day the courting began, was a beautiful one. The honeysuckle vines, wrapped around the church's white picket fence, let off a fine smell that yelled "spring!" The temperature was pleasant and the sermon, "praise the

Lawd," wasn't too long. The choir sung and the mothers on the Women's Auxiliary shouted on cue as if the choir director had conducted it as such. It was a great day for a function, and for courting.

"Did you see Sister Campbell hollering and carrying on like that?" said Anna. "The Spirit really moved her today."

"You can say that again. It moved her right up and down the church. And when you thought she was finish, back again," said Ida Mae. "It took all three of her sons and the whole usher board to calm her down. I know Barbara was shame, having her momma screamin' and carryin' on like that."

"Barbara told me that her momma and Sister Dawson take turns tryin' to outshout each other. That if one of them shouts the first Sunday and cleared an entire pew, then you could rest assured the second Sunday the other would shout, not quittin' until two had been cleared."

"Who you tellin'? Sittin' by either of 'em is just askin' for a bruisin'. When you see that hand start to goin' up in the air and wavin' 'round, you know it's just a matter of time 'fore the dancin' starts. You'd think she'd been down to the Rusty Nail the way she carries on."

"Ida Mae, stop it! Somebody's gonna hear you."

"I'm speakin' the truth, and the truth shall set

you free," said Ida Mae, waving her hand through the air and throwing her head back as if the Spirit had hit her.

Ida Mae had been Anna's best friend since they were li'l girls playing beauty shop. And like in that place where women are being pampered, there was nothing they wouldn't tell each other. Anna kept Ida Mae tame; Ida Mae made Anna feel as if she wasn't.

People seem to enjoy when you play on the edge. They keep all eyes focused upon you, in hopes of witnessing the moment of your fall. Eyes were forever upon Ida Mae, for she was as near to the edge as they came. If it could be done, Ida Mae had done it, was in the process of doing it, or was thinking about how she could do it without getting caught. All the same, Anna could rest assured that as soon as the deed was done, she would be the first—or the second, as the case might be—to hear about it, and that's the way it had been for years.

"Ol' Clayton Jamison was just a-hummin' 'round my honey jar last night at the Nail," said Ida Mae, while biting into the drumstick she had in her basket. "I told him if he had half a tooth in his mouth, I might just let him, but since he don't to take his stinger and move on way from me."

"Ida Mae, why you so mean?" said Anna, teasingly. "That boy has been chasin' you for as long as he's been able to stand on two legs, and you've always been mean to him."

"Anna, long as we been friends, you still don't know nothin' 'bout menfolk, do you? All this time, I guess I ain't taught you nothin'. You gots to be mean to 'em if you want 'em to keep your taste in they mouth. It's like a challenge for 'em, see. You know they out there tellin' all they bizness to they no-'count li'l friends. Once they done that, then they gotta keep after you, 'cuz if they don't get you, then they friends don't ever let 'em live it down. Why? 'Cuz that's how menfolk is. The meaner you are to 'em, the more they think it's worth it when they finally get you."

"You mean you gonna let Clayton Jamison . . . ?"

"Hell, nah! I wouldn't let him within a whiff's distance of a cow patty. But he don't know that, and that's what keeps him after me. And that's what keeps my glass full at the Nail. Speakin' of, you wanna li'l drank?"

"No, thank you. I got some lemonade that Momma made and . . ."

"Anna, what I'm gonna do witchu?" said Ida Mae, pulling out a bottle of gin. "I mean a drank, honey. A real drank, not no goddamn lemonade. And definitely not that grape juice they tryin' to pass off for wine up in that there church house."

"You're goin' to get us both in trouble, Ida Mae.

Put that bottle away. If my momma sees you with that, she's goin' to skin our hides; then you know she's goin' to tell your people and you'll get torn up again."

"I might get it, but if I do, I wanna have a li'l fun meanwhiles. Here's to you, precious." Ida Mae raised the bottle to her lips and took a hearty swig. Her face soured for a minute and then slowly returned to normal. "Ain't bad. Ain't bad at all. Come on, Anna, have a taste. Just a little one. It's Sunday. One Spirit deserves another."

Anna, looking around to make sure nobody was eyeing them, took the bottle and poured a peach pit's worth into her jar of lemonade. She shook the jar to mix it, then took a swig.

Ida Mae and Anna sat there under that old oak tree near the creek that breezy Sunday afternoon, long ago, talking. Ida Mae told tales that Anna never could decide if they were true or not, but she would always listen, gladly. Anna would live the life of each of Ida Mae's stories to the fullest, if nothing more than in her mind. And as far as Anna was concerned, as long as she could be a part of that, that proved plenty.

As the day went on, the lemonade disappeared and Anna was getting friendlier, as her sipping seemed to soothe her.

"That's really nice," said Anna taking the last sip from the jar.

"My cousin, Lester, in Detroit—I think you met Lester one time when he was last down here—well, he says gin is the 'preferred' drink up north."

"No, Ida Mae. I don't mean the gin, though it is nice. I mean Joseph Thomas over there. Don't look. Okay, now. Look."

"Girrrl, I know you must be drunk."

"Maybe I am. Maybe I'm not."

Joseph had been walking back and forth along the creek and Anna had been watching him while Ida Mae's tales carried the storyline. Of course at the time, she wasn't a wife and she certainly didn't know he would be a husband, at least not hers. It was just a crush, is what I'm told, a church function crush.

"Don't you think he looks handsome, with those bowlegs and all?" Anna said, smiling and swaying on that blanket like she could hear her favorite hymn playing in the distance from the now-empty church.

"Hell, nah! He's trouble, trouble, I tell you. Don't evah trust no boy with no bowlegs. They get 'round more than a fever in winter, and that's too much for my taste," said Ida Mae, finishing off her bottle of gin and pulling out yet another from what seemed to be an endless supply. "Now if you wanna

*be happy, stay way from bowlegged mens. And any-
how, you know Missus Anderson would have a con-
niption fit if that boy came a-callin' on you. He ain't
nothin' but a heathen. Always been a heathen. Ain't
gonna be nothin' but a heathen."*

"No such a thing. He's sweet."

*"Precious, melons is sweet. Bowlegged mens
ain't."*

"Ida Mae, melons are sweet. Not is sweet."

*"Is or ain't, Miz Proper. Fine by me, but that boy
ain't worth the strain on your eyes you usin' to look
at him."*

*"Who says? I think he'd suit me just fine. He's
got a job down at the mill and makin' good money.
A girl could do worse for herself. Besides, who are
you to talk? You sure ain't no candidate for the
Women's Auxiliary."*

*Anna took a swig from the new bottle of gin, and
just as she was bringing it away from her lips . . .*

*"Anna! Anna! Lorda be! You put that devil water
down this instant, young lady." It was her mother,
Missus Anderson, standing rooted next to the oak
tree that only moments ago served as shade. But no
amount of leaves could shield Anna from the heat
of her mother's stare. Anna knew she was in for it.
Every time she heard the phrase* young lady, *she
knew she had it coming.*

"But Momma, I . . ."

" 'Momma, I? Momma, I' nothing. It's too late to be
'Momma, I'-ing. You should have thought of
'Momma, I' before you let that filth pass your lips.
Now that's what you should've done. Being as you
didn't, you're going to get it when you get home,
young lady. Now come with me," said Missus Anderson, pulling Anna up by the sleeve of her dress. "I
know this is your doings, Ida Mae Ramsey, and don't
think I'm not gonna tell Corene when I see her."

"But Missus Anderson . . ."

"Don't say another word. Not another single word,
Ida Mae, or I'll have the mind to take a branch from
this tree and tan those big old legs of yours right here
and now. The good Lord knows a switch couldn't do
nothing to them. Now, come on, Anna."

Missus Anderson and Ida Mae had had many
rounds of this sort. Ida Mae knew it was hopeless,
so she didn't say another word. Not another word.

Anna didn't get a hiding that day, just sent to her
room, "to think about what you've done." Ida Mae
did, but she was used to it. Getting put on "restriction, young lady" hurt Anna, but not as much as
her knowing Joseph Thomas saw her being pulled
away by her own momma.

Gram Anderson was a gracious lady, "refined and
dignified," it's been said, but she didn't mind shaming you in front of people if you happened to get

out of line. To her, it wasn't about shaming you, but "setting you straight." I've heard good stories about Gram Anderson. Early on, Momma used to say how she wished Gram was around now, because she would know what to do. She would know how to handle Poppa, and she would make everything all right for me. But Gram isn't around now. It's just Momma and me. Just us.

... Sometimes I think it's just me and this baby. I find myself talking to her. I need to talk to someone, even if they can't talk back, maybe *because* they can't talk back. For the time being, it is just this baby and me. Just us. Maybe God sent me this baby so I wouldn't feel helpless ...

We were up and about early this morning. Never got to sleep, really. After Poppa had finished doing his do, he just rolled back over and was asleep before Momma could even mumble the words *have a good night's rest*. She just lay there with the quilt pulled up enough so that I was covered and warm. Every time Poppa moved or rolled from his left to right side, she would hold her breath, hoping he wouldn't wake up, praying he would stay asleep until it would be a reasonable time for her to get out of bed to begin her day. At long last, that time had come.

It was still before day, and Momma knew Poppa would be getting up soon to go talk to James about him and Clariece raising me. Momma and I started out in the yard. March mist covered the Johnson grass, making the surroundings heavenly, though things otherwise seemed far from it.

"It's gonna be a fine day today. It's God's day, li'l Lisa. Nothin' bad is comin' on God's day."

We picked up the kindling for the stove and went back inside, careful not to let the screen door slam behind. Momma lit the stove, and the early morning chill that visited our house in the night was soon replaced by warmth. Even though my fate was to be decided today, in a matter of hours, Momma always kept me warm, protected; no kindling was needed for that.

"You want to help me make some biscuits? You know biscuits are your favorite," says Momma. "You move like the dickens ever'time we have biscuits." This time the words came through a soothing hum so as no voice would wake the morning from its sleep or wake the worry on her brow. "I know you enjoy them smothered with butter and hot maple syrup. Why don't we fix them up like you like them. Today is your day."

Nothing is more soothing than a mother's hum.

Momma kept the big tin of flour near the stove. Every time she bent down to get a cupful, I could feel myself moving nearer to her heart. She would get as many cups as necessary to feed the seven mouths she had to feed and the eighth one that Poppa wanted Clariece to feed. After she sifted all the flour needed, she sprinkled two handfuls along the kitchen table so as the dough wouldn't stick.

She kneaded.

She did all this with a gentle ease, care going into each movement, dough taking shape under her hands, between her fingers, each joint becoming familiar. The head of the Mason jar shaped the biscuits to a perfect size, and from one came many, all by the same hands, each receiving no more and no less dough. She took the leftover scrap of dough, rolling it, and made one biscuit for herself. It wasn't as pretty as the others, but would taste just as good, all the same.

When Momma was cooking, there was always a dishrag nearby. It served as a close friend, when needed. The dishrag was kept within arm's reach, never really being used for much, just something to fill those moments when the next instant was forming but hadn't quite risen. A touch here, a dab there, a moment to breathe. Wipe the sweat from the corner of her eye before it presented a sting. It took her to the next step, the time between thought and creation. Being the only woman around, she needed a friend, something to hold on to, when holding on to anyone seemed so far from possible.

As Momma put the biscuits in the stove, a noise came from her and Poppa's bedroom. It didn't startle her. She was used to it.

"You hear that, li'l Lisa?" she says, smiling like a young girl meeting a young boy for the first time— after it had been decided that it was all right to like boys. "That's your Poppa in there snorin' up a breeze. I'm surprised he doesn't snore his nose off. He must have rolled over on his back. His mouth tends to fall open when he sleeps on his back. Now, I know it's loud as can be, but you'll get used to it in time where it won't even bother you so. He's just sleepin' real good, that's all. He needs his rest. Rest'll do him good. The smell of these here biscuits oughta fill up that nose of his in a minute."

As Momma took out the first batch of biscuits and put them in the lined wicker basket that when not in use hung on the kitchen wall, the ol' house rooster, perched on the barbed wire fencepost in the yard, crowed and she knew our private time together was nearing an end. Poppa's morning sound, too, would soon wake the house.

"Junior?" screams Poppa from the bedroom. "Boy, you up? Junior? Junior, get up and watch the house. You gonna have to be in charge a thangs 'round here today."

"J. T., why don't you let the boy sleep? He works hard all week long and there's really nothin' for him to do till it's time for Sunday school," says Momma as Poppa comes into the kitchen. She piles biscuits on a plate, placing it at his place at the table, hoping the smell of the melting butter mixed with the maple syrup would tempt his taste buds, moisten his mouth, soften his words.

"He ain't the only one who works hard 'round here," says Poppa, taking the butter and syrup from

Momma and putting more on his plate. "If I'm up, then he needs to be up, too. I'm gonna be gone for most of the day and somebody needs to be 'round here to look after thangs. Junior?! Junior, are you up, boy? Don't let me have to call up in there again."

"Yessir! I'm up."

"Then why don't I hear no movin' 'round up in there, then? Get the molasses out ya ass, boy, and get on in here. Hear?"

"J. T., please. It's Sunday. Don't wake the rest of them. He's up. Give him a minute," says Momma, grabbing hold of the dishrag and walking over to the sink. She had her back to him when she said it. She didn't want to see what he was thinking and she didn't want to upset him. Not today. She knew too much was depending on it.

Junior came out of the bedroom and sat down across from Poppa.

Junior is my oldest brother, and being Momma's first-born makes him almost as close to her as I am. He works at the lumber mill, too. He's mostly quiet, keeping to himself as much as possible. He knew what it was like to go out to the chicken coop and be gentle when it came to taking the eggs from the nest. Junior didn't rightly understand why he had to get up, but he wasn't about to question it. For him, sleep was always light anyhow.

"I wants you to watch the place today, you hear? See that your brothers minds ya momma and gets off to church. I needs you to stay 'round the house."

Poppa says this without looking at Junior or without missing the rythmn in which he sops up the syrup with his biscuits.

"But, Poppa . . ." Before Junior can continue his thought, Momma gently but firmly places one hand on his shoulder and with the other puts a plate of biscuits in front of him. "Thank you," he says.

"You're welcome," says Momma, again walking to the sink, grabbing the dishrag that always waited on her.

Junior enjoyed church. It was the one place he felt as if he wasn't being watched. For six days of the week, whether at work or home, he felt eyes were always on top of him, waiting for an opportunity for their stares to be translated into words or actions; even when they blinked, a sun-cast image of Junior was burned into that instant of darkness. There was no rest for him, for once those eyes opened again, they only stared harder to make sure the image was the same as before and nothing was missed.

"I wahn't plannin' on takin' this trip," says Poppa, almost as if spitting the words at Momma, "and it's gonna throw me off for the rest of the week. 'Sides, you almost too old to be runnin' off to some church ever' Sunday. You a man now, and God can't do nothin' for ya ya can't do for ya own self."

Poppa pushes away from the table, throwing his napkin on the empty plate. Momma picked up his plate. Taking his napkin, she dabbed at the beads of sweat strung above her lip.

"Something to drink, J. T.?" says Momma, to Poppa's stiff, uninterested back.

"Nah."

Junior sat, watching, picking at his biscuits, flake by flake, layer by layer. It was like a routine that everyone knew but not necessarily enjoyed.

"I'll be back 'fore dark," says Poppa, walking out the screen door again, it slamming behind him. This wakes my brother, Leselle, who starts screaming.

"I'll try and get him back to sleep," Junior says, picking up his plate of half-eaten biscuits and putting it by the sink.

"Thank you," says Momma, as she nibbles from his plate, more for my sake than for her own.

. . . How I remember the old days. It all seemed so simple then. Maybe it wasn't. Maybe I just looked at things differently. Maybe I was looked at differently. So many maybes to hold on to. If not for "maybe," God only knows what might be . . .

"Ida Mae," said Joseph, tipping his hat.

"I don't know why you sayin' no 'Ida Mae' to me, Joseph Thomas. You know it's Anna you wants to talk to."

"Ida Mae, stop it," said Anna in a whisper that escapes her teeth, trying, yet failing, to keep a straight face.

"I'm just tryin' to be polite, is all," he said, turning to Anna. "You lookin' right nice today, Anna. That dress sho 'nough suits you."

"Why, thank you. I . . ."

"She look nice ever' day. Who you think you foolin', fool? 'Be polite.' Joseph Thomas, I'd like to know where you got that notion. You haven't been polite a day in your natural-born life, and now—now you 'spect us to carry the notion that you tryin' to 'be polite.' Nigra, please!"

"Ida Mae!" said Anna, pinching Ida Mae.

"Ow! Girl! Why you do that. . . ?"

"Well, I see you fine ladies are busy. I'll just be moseyin' on 'long."

"You do that. And you! Don't be pinchin' me like that. You know I hate that. It minds me of yo' momma. She's always pinchin' me. You turnin' more and more like her ever' day."

While Ida Mae was going on about the pinching, Joseph was walking away, and Anna's eyes marked every step as closely as if she were following them wherever they would lead. She couldn't even hear Ida Mae anymore. All she could think about was Joseph Thomas and missing her chance at him once again.

"You see that? You see that? You made him uneasy and shooed him away," said Anna, pulling her feet out of Riley's Creek.

"So what? He ain't no kind of catch. He must've

followed us out here. Ol' bowlegged rascal. Don't nobody come out to this here creek but us. Don't you think it's strange that he just happened upon us out here? Use your head for more than a hat-rack." Ida Mae said all this in one breath, yet never took her legs out of the water. Her already ample calves appeared double in size under the water and she liked the way they looked, the way the water wrapped around them like the finest of stockings from up north. "If you ask me, he followed us out here hopin' to get a sneak peek."

"No!" said Anna otherwise . . .

"Yes."

"No!"

"Yes. Two nice-lookin' girls like ourselves, out here by our lonesome. I bet he thought he could see a little somethin' to go back and tell his triflin' hang-out buddies about."

"Why he need to come out here to do that, when you show it around at the juke joint anyhow?"

"Anna!" Ida Mae pulled her legs up out of the water and started running toward Anna, who took off running, laughing and screaming "no" all the way. Ida Mae hiked up her dress and let her calves do their thing. Before long, they fell to the ground, giggling and rolling around in the clover, wishes waiting to be claimed.

Breathing heavily, Ida Mae said, "He didn't come out here to see me, Anna. He came to see you."

"No such a thing. Joseph Thomas could have any girl in Welty County, and any neighborin' one if he had a mind to do it. Why would he want to look at me?"

"Ain't no need in tryin' to question the truth. All I have to say is watch yaself. I ain't gonna be there all the time to keep the wicked away. Speaking of, it's near 'bout dark. You'd better get on home 'fore Missus Anderson come lookin' for you."

Grabbing an old dandelion, Anna said, "Ida Mae? You think you ever gonna get married?"

"I don't know. I 'spect so. To tell the truth, I guess I haven't put much thought to it. I don't rightly see myself with nobody—no one somebody. But I s'pose anythang could happen. Why?"

"Just askin'."

"You?"

"Yeah. I think I'd like to," said Anna, closing her eyes and blowing into the dandelion. The wind took each of the seeds and they vanished, floating over the water into the beginning of night. Where they'd land was left for the imagination.

2

Momma had been nervous all day. We spent most of it back and forth between the bathroom. It's near night and Poppa isn't back yet from talking to Uncle James.

We went to church. Momma rocked back and forth in the pew, but the choir wasn't even singing. She just rocked. She rubbed me as she did, telling me over and over again that I had nothing to worry about.

"Ever'thing is gonna be fine, li'l Lisa. You needn't worry one bit about that." Though she was saying it to me, the congregation could be heard saying, "yes" and "well" and "say that," verifying the truth in what had been said. Would that it were only that easy. She kept right on telling me it was going to be fine. She was right, I needn't worry about a thing, for as she sat in that third pew rocking, as if trying to put a baby to sleep, I knew she was worrying enough for the both of us.

After church, the walk home was tiring. Junior usually was the one who ran the train, making the boys stay in line. But as Poppa had told him, he stayed at home, leaving Momma with her hands full.

"Momma, I think Stanley's momma was sad."

"Why's that, Leselle?"

" 'Cause she was cryin' and all those men had to come and take her outside."

"That's 'cause she was shoutin', fool."

"Edward James Joseph!" Momma shouted. "What did I tell you about callin' people a fool? Now tell your brother you didn't mean it."

"But I did mean it, Momma. Any fool can tell you when a woman shouts, she's feelin' the Spirit."

"I ain't no fool, either," screamed Leselle. He and Edward had to share a bed, keeping them constantly at each other's throat and keeping Momma on guard. Today, she didn't have it in her to keep up with them. Her mind was elsewhere. But being Momma, she tried to stitch things together.

"No, Leselle, you're not a fool. You see, Stanley's momma . . . well, you see, she had what we call the Spirit. She was happy. I know sometimes it can look like they're sad because they're cryin', but it's a good thing, what they're feelin'. It's hard to understand at first, but you'll soon come to realize it's a good thing.

"I remember the first time I was old enough to go to church with your gram; we sat up on the front pew. It was an Easter Sunday, so ever'body was dressed to the nines in their new clothes, tryin' to show out for ever'body else and passin' judgment along the way.

"The choir sang and the voices were as strong as a soul set free, makin' sounds like that of angels. And me and your gram were sittin' there. She was clappin' in time and everthin' seemed fine. Then a while later, I looked up and your gram started cryin', slowly at first. But as the singin' continued, it soon became somethin' much more than tears.

"Whenever they would get to the end of the song, the pastor, because he could see the congregation was feelin' it, would get up and tell the soloist and the choir to keep on singin'. So the piano player would start up playin' again and the choir would join in singin' on time, gettin' louder with each re-frain. Gram would get worse, and before long it got wheres they had to take her out.

"I sat there by my lonesome and I got scared, and the preacher kept makin' the choir sing more, and I started cryin'. The people on our pew scooted next to me, puttin' their arms around me because they thought I was feelin' the Spirit, too. But I was just afraid and mad at that mean ol' preacher for doin' this to Gram. I wasn't feelin' the Spirit at all. I was just scared, like you were."

"I wasn't scared," said Leselle in defense of himself.

"No, Leselle. I'm sure you weren't. Big boys like you don't get afraid."

"But if Gram was happy and feelin' the Spirit, why did they take her out? Why didn't they let her stay in and be happy?"

"That's a good question, Leselle. I wish I knew the answer. Maybe you can get too much of it, so they have to take you out, so . . . I don't know, Leselle. I don't know. It seems like if it was truly a good thing, they wouldn't take you out, would they?"

"Do you sometimes feel the Spirit now, Momma?"

"Yes, Leselle. Sometimes I do. But there's nothin' for you to be afraid of. It's just the Spirit, it won't hurt you."

"Why don't I ever see mens gettin' the Spirit?"

"Well, I'm sure men feel it, too. It's just they show it in a different way."

"See, Edward. I told you, I weren't no fool," said Leselle, plucking Edward's ear and running off down the road toward home. Leon and Leo didn't say a word the whole time. They each walked on Momma's side, holding her hand, with me in the middle.

When we got back home, Momma began to fix

supper. She always did most of it the night before or in the morning before she went to church; that way when she got home, she could try to relax, if just for a moment.

"You need some help, Momma."

"No, thank you, Junior. There's not that much left to do." Momma stopped for a moment and looked at Junior. "You know your Poppa doesn't mean no harm, don't you? You're just the next one in line and he's proud of you. He wants you to grow up to be a good man, that's all."

"I know, Momma. I know," he said, leaving the kitchen and going out onto the porch. Momma looked at him through the kitchen window. He sat on the step below where Poppa's rocker sat. With his hand, he rocked it back and forth, every now and again taking that very hand and placing it under the chair's curved leg, stopping it in midrock.

. . . Ida Mae, Ida Mae, Ida Mae.

There's so much comfort in just writing your name. What memories a name can conjure.

I'm standing steady while time moves on. I sit here at times fantasizing about how exciting your life must be. I see you walk down streets I've never even seen. I know you're dressing up, too, looking good every step of the way. What a time you must be having. You always knew how to have a good time.

I wake each morning, fearful, waiting for an

answer or sign from above. Today, the answer isn't coming from the heavens but from some thirty miles away, which, from here, is like the same distance.

I have faith in the goodness of the unknown, but the devil can still your faith. I've never thought of the devil as a woman, but today, I do. Clariece—I'm sure you remember her—is trying to place a claim on a soul that she has no rights to . . .

As darkness settles around our house, Momma knows Poppa should be back at any time. She keeps finding reasons to walk by the door or go outside. The night is silent except for the locusts playing tag in the cornfield. How happy they sound. Momma turned off the lights and lit candles. When Poppa arrived, she didn't want him to see anything, good or bad, in her face. As she stands in the door, she's startled by a scream.

"Momma! Edward called me a fool again!"

"Tattletale! Tattletale, hang yo' britches on a rusty nail."

"I ain't."

"Yes, you are."

"Ain't neither."

"Both of you just stop it," Junior screams in from the porch, where he's reading his Bible. Leselle and Edward become silent. Junior, too, is waiting to be taken off duty, waiting for that figure to come walking through the gate, yet having no idea what to expect from it once it does.

The twins, Leo and Leon, are always quiet. They had themselves and never really needed for much more. Poppa would sometimes scream at them just because I think they scared him as much as he scared them. He didn't like that. Momma never had to worry about them, for they had each other. They were the last born and are probably the reason Poppa is turned off of me. He wasn't expecting two, and when they came, he blamed Momma. It was then that he decided she couldn't have no more children. In some odd way, it was as if Leo and Leon knew this, and for that reason, they were pleased to have each other—unlike Edward and Leselle, who are more than two years apart and act like they can't stand the breath that made each of them live.

Edward and Leselle often fight the twins, but they're no match for this duo. In their silence is strength.

They say Momma was really big when she was carrying the twins, so much so that Gram had to come and stay, which really kept Poppa on his heels. They say Gram was the only one who could actually keep him in check, which is nice to hear, but it doesn't change what's going on now, as we wait for Poppa to return from speaking to Uncle James and Auntie Clariece.

"Ida Mae, I'm so nervous. Momma'll be here any minute, and you know how she and Joe are."

"I know exactly how they are: like two porcupines tryin' to make love. One is busy tryin' to stick but gettin' stuck at the same time," said Ida Mae, taking a chug from her bottle.

"Ida Mae, you are a fool," said Anna, wobbling over to a chair at the kitchen table.

"You best not let Missus Anderson hear you usin' that word; she'll give you a hidin', pregnant or not."

"You know Momma too well."

At just that moment, a knock came at the door. It was Gram Anderson. Usually a knock precedes an entrance, but with Gram, a knock and entrance proved to be one.

"Hello! Is anybody gonna come help an old woman or do I have to carry these bags another twenty miles? You know ten steps equals a mile to an old woman."

"Momma, you're early," said Anna, trying to get up from her chair. She was still months away from giving birth but was "big beyond belief."

"Well, what you want me to do, turn around, go back, stand on the trail a li'l while, then come back later when it's more convenient for you?"

"No, ma'am. Junior! No, ma'am, now is fine. Junior?! Your gram is here. Come fetch her bags, please. No, ma'am. See, I was gonna have Junior meet you at the cross section, but I didn't expect you so soon."

"Well, sooner or later, I'm here now, so there's no need in carrying on and fretting about that subject one moment more. Now, Junior, be careful with that bag," said Gram Anderson, almost screaming, "because I have a present in there for you and I don't want it to get messed up." She pinched Junior's cheek and handed him a five folded in fours. She always gave Junior large sums of money, as if that could make up for other things that she couldn't rightly control—money for time served.

Junior knew Gram Anderson always sounded as if she were in a bad mood, but she never was. She had no reason to be. She was her own woman and answered to no one. She did as she pleased, when she pleased, and what pleased her now was to be with her daughter. Even the best mothers need to know they're still needed.

"I just saw you two Sundays ago, and it looks like you've gotten three times bigger," said Gram Anderson, walking around her only child like she was a prize sow at the Mississippi State Fair.

"Ain't she big, Missus Anderson? Big as the house she standin' in, and I tell you . . ."

"Who asked you, Ida Mae?"

"Nobody. But . . ."

"Right. Nobody. Then mind your beeswax and

keep your opinions to yourself. If I want to know what you're thinking, I'll tell you. 'Big as the house she standin' in.' Now what kind of sense does that make, Ida Mae? 'Big as the house she standin' in,' huh? Now come on over here, baby, and let Momma feel that stomach." Gram Anderson ran her hands along Anna's stomach and then put her ear on her belly as if it might speak. "Lorda be. The way it's sitting and the sound of it, I think it's twins."

"I told you! I told you, Anna. I told you it was gonna be twins. Sure as I'm standin' here, I said it," shouted Ida Mae, slapping her hands together. Gram Anderson gave her a look, putting a dent in Ida Mae's huge grin. "But I did tell her."

"Well, Ida Mae, it seems, for once—thank God for small favors—you're right. It's definitely twins. Junior! Stop snooping in that bag now. I'll give you the present when I'm good and ready, and not a moment before. Until then, stop snooping. Curiosity killed the cat, and what he found couldn't bring him back."

"Yes'm," screamed a guilty Junior from the bedroom.

"Momma, now how did you know he was in your bag?"

"Because he's a child and I'm a mother and mothers know things. And one thing I know is that you're carrying twins, so . . ." And with the swiftest *of transitions, Gram looked down at Anna's ankles. Raising Anna's dress a notch, she said, "Lorda be, look at those tree trunks. I've seen trees with years of rings thinner than this. That no-good, trifling husband of yourn has been working you to death. Figures. Well, not to worry, Momma is here now, so just sit yourself down and rest these stumps.*

"If Ida Mae was of any account, she would be doing something to help out around here. But it's evident to me she doesn't see fit to do so." Gram Anderson took Anna's apron from around her belly and began cleaning up. "Junior! Come from out of there. I told you I'd give it to you later. Now where is Edward and Leselle? Those little mannish devils. Hiding, huh? I guess Gram is going to have to steal some sugar if she wants some. Well, we'll just see how that is when I start pulling out presents . . ."

Leselle and Edward came running out of the room to the sound of that. Gram Anderson had taken over. Ida Mae and Anna watched in amazement.

That was how Anna knew Leo and Leon would be twins and from then on never doubted it for a minute. She was glad her mother was there because it would be easier to tell Joseph the news of two. Ida Mae wasn't allowed around the house when he was there, so she wasn't going to be able to help.

But Gram Anderson knew how to handle Poppa, and usually it took only one glance.

The secret present Gram brought for Junior was a Bible. It belonged to her mother and her mother before. Its cover was still hard and sturdy; the pages, fragile to the touch. It seemed only right it should come from Gram. Junior would spend many a day reading that Bible. Gram left many fond memories in that home, but the Bible was something that could be held, something that wasn't Joseph's property.

That gift would be the last from Gram Anderson. She passed away shortly after that visit. There's no such thing as sudden death, but that's how it looked back then. She would never know if her prediction of twins was right, though time would prove it true. Even death bears a life of its own.

Anna took the news as any child would after being cut off from its lifeline, when that had seemed like such a distant possibility.

"It's nice out," says Momma, joining Junior out on the porch.

"Yeah, since those two shut up in there, things seem right peaceful, for a change."

"Sometimes I enjoy hearin' them fight. It makes me know they're alive."

"I guess. But then I guess it depends on what

they're fighting about," says Junior, looking back down at his Bible.

"Is there enough light out here for you?"

"I can see awright."

"Yes. I'm sure you can." Momma gets up and goes back into the house. She peeks in on the boys. Leselle and Edward are asleep. Leo and Leon are pretending to be, but as soon as Momma opens the door, they look up at her.

"You boys aren't asleep yet?" she says in a half whisper.

"No, ma'am," says Leon. One always speaks and the other is silent, as if each knew when and which answer was his to claim. "We're not sleepy just yet."

"All right. But don't stay up too late now. You boys need your rest."

"Yes, ma'am," says Leo. Momma starts to walk away. "Momma?"

"Yes, Leo?"

"We love you." He says this in such a truthful and youthful way that I feel a loose knot pass my body, tightening as it sits for a second near Momma's heart before making its way up and lodging, for a restless rest, in her throat.

"I love you, too. The both of you," says the knot, as she turns and walks out the door. As the first tear begins to roll down her cheek, there is Poppa standing at the screen door. "Joe?"

"It's done," he says. No remorse or pleasure

wrapped his statement—no sign of anything. He gave her nothing more than that. "It's done." He said it, then went to the kitchen and sat in his place at the table, waiting for Momma to follow behind to fix his plate. Junior stood in stillness looking at Momma, and I felt that single tear fall, bringing an echo around me certain to last generations to come.

... This morning I feel like a piece of driftwood, wading to see where the waves will lead me. I know it won't be far. The pond where I play is only so big, the banks, so near . . .

The next morning, Poppa didn't say a word. He just got up, ate, then went on off to work, Junior following closely but silently behind. Momma sent the boys off to their schooling, then herself off to work.

She always went in to Miss Janie's on Mondays to wash up from the week past. The walk was always a pleasant one as she walked off her worries. Miss Janie lived across the tracks near town, which is where most of the white folks lived, at least the acceptable ones. Momma had worked for Miss Janie since Junior was born and Miss Janie had always been good people. Now Momma worked only once a week because there really wasn't much to do. Miss Janie really had her come in mainly to keep her company, another person to fill up that big, lonely, picket fence–wrapped house on the hill.

Poppa got mad when Momma's days were cut back, even though he had been against her working in the first place. Soon after her days were cut to one, Junior started working at the mill, and that seemed to make everything sit right with Poppa.

Junior never did get to go to the school that was set up for the colored children by a few of the colored families. Somewhere down the line through the "goodness" of white folks, these families learned to read and write and figure. Junior wouldn't even have learned how to read had it not been for Miss Janie, and of course Momma, encouraging him and providing lessons while Poppa was away from the house. Miss Janie was a friend to our family even though Poppa disliked her so. He never stepped foot on a single blade of Miss Janie's property. He loved the money Momma brought in from working, but hated her being somewhere outside of a world familiar to him.

"Good morning, Miss Janie," says Momma, putting down her bag near the back door.

"Anna! Anna! Come quick. I've been waiting for you. There's someone in the house, Anna. I know there's someone in the house," says Miss Janie, running to the back door when she saw us coming up the walk. She looked like she'd seen a ghost. She *looked* like a ghost. "They know, Anna. They know, and they're here to get me and lynch me. They want to lynch me. The devil sent them."

"No, ma'am. There's nobody here," says Momma,

trying to soothe her. "Let me make you some tea. That'll calm your nerves."

"You calling me a liar? All the things I've done for you. I've been good to you, Anna, and you're going to stand there looking in my face and call me a liar?"

"No, ma'am. No such thing. I just don't think anybody is in the house, but I'll have a look-see if it will make you feel better."

"Please do, Anna. I know they've found out and are coming to lynch me."

Since Miss Janie had been living in that house by herself, her imagination had taken the best of her, running faster than her mind had breath for, as only time alone can cause. Every sound from a floor-board or the wind beating a shutter rang through this house, made for many, but lived in now by only one. The house had not been redecorated since Momma first stepped in it. Time stood still for Miss Janie while the world outside of these ten rooms pressed on.

Her son had moved on to Atlanta with his wife, Sarah, and she wouldn't go to live with them when they sent for her. She told Momma a whiles back that she wasn't going to leave her husband's house to be where she wasn't wanted. She said being lonely was better than being unwanted.

"It's that wife of his. She's evil—evil, I tell you. I knew it from the very beginning. A mother knows, you know."

"Yes, ma'am, I know."

"From the moment I laid eyes on that gal . . . that . . . that philanderer, I knew she was gonna take my boy away from me, and as sure as I said it, she did. She put a hex on him. That's exactly what she did. No telling what she's got him doing over there in Sodom. And I'm sure she's ringered my sweet, sweet Beth into this somehow. They were both just the sweetest of children. Weren't they, Anna?"

"Yes, ma'am. They sure were. Couldn't have asked for better chilren."

"Anna? Anna, make me some tea. Could you, please? Chamomile. I need some tea to soothe my nerves."

"I think that's a fine idea, Miss Janie."

Miss Janie's daughter, Elizabeth, had moved up north to Boston with her husband and she rarely got to see her. So for the last nine years, Momma has been coming and watching as Miss Janie slips away.

"Miss Janie, I've looked up and down and there's nobody in the house," says Momma, putting down the tea on the coffee table.

"Did you check the attic?"

"Yes, ma'am."

"How about the closets?"

"Yes, ma'am. Checked every one and there's not a soul to be found."

"Then they've left, Anna. They were here, I tell

you. They'll be back. They know. They're coming to lynch me in the town square, so everybody can laugh and ridicule me."

"No need in worryin' about it now, Miss Janie. I'm here and I'm not goin' to let nothin' happen to you."

Each Monday, the story topped the one from the week before, but Momma would wash up, sit for a spell, and then be on her way. By the time Momma had finished all the work left for her and was ready-ing to leave, Miss Janie had usually calmed down after taking one of her "magic pills" and playtime would be over. But not today.

"Miss Janie, I'm finished. I cooked you some sup-per. I wrapped it up in tinfoil and left it in the oven so it'll stay warm till you're ready for it. I'm gonna be going now," says Momma, standing, watching Miss Janie sitting in her rocker and looking straight up at the ceiling as if looking through it to heaven.

"Anna, have I been a bad girl? Is that why you're leaving?" says Miss Janie, balling up her handker-chief in her liver-spotted hands.

"No, ma'am. It's just, you see, I've done all the washin' up and . . . and I cooked your supper like I always do. I have to get on home while there's still daylight and take care of my family."

"You have a family?"

"Yes, ma'am. You know I have a family, Miss Janie. You remember Junior and my other boys."

"Where are they, Anna? Tell me where they are."

"They're at home, Miss Janie. They're at home waitin' on me."

"Home?"

"Yes, ma'am. They're at home."

"You can't go. You can't go, because when you leave, they're going to get me. They're in the house, I tell you. That evil woman in Atlanta sent them here to get me. I saw the envelope again today. Her messenger sent it. Been sending one practically every day."

"What envelope, Miss Janie?"

"Over there. I hid it from them so her spies wouldn't see her instructions. I put it in there," says Miss Janie, pointing with trembling finger toward the cedar chest across the room. "I put all the important things in that chest so I can keep a watchful eye on it. They're in this house, Anna. She's sent them. I know she did. And they want to take me to the town square to tar and feather me. No. Not tar and feather me. No, they want to lash me, that's it."

Momma walks over to the cedar chest and opens it. Inside were different things that looked as if they were thrown in in a hurry. The good silver. Family albums. Miss Janie's favorite crocheted quilt. Baby clothes. Then the envelopes. Momma picks up one of the envelopes and under it is a photograph of Miss Janie's boy, Pete. It was his wedding photograph, but his wife Sarah's face had been torn out of the picture.

"The devil, she is. As sure as I'm standing here today, she's the devil. She sent that letter through her spies. I know she did it. My boy wouldn't do this to me. Petey wouldn't. Not to his mother. She's the devil and she's hexed him. That's what she's done. She's from Louisiana, you know. They do crazy things over there. Voodoo. She's put some potion on him, and her spies are going to poison me. They're here, I tell you," says Miss Janie, coming over to the cedar chest. "When they come, I want you to make sure they don't touch the chest. They want to rob me of these treasures. But you've got to fight them, Anna!"

Momma opens the top envelope and pulls out the letter.

Dearest Mother,

I wish there were an easier way to address this matter than through a missive as such, but Sarah and I have given it a great deal of consideration, feeling it best if you are brought here to Atlanta so that a better eye can be kept on you. What do you think about that?

I've also discussed this matter with Elizabeth and we both agree that at your age, it is vital to your well-being that you be nearer to the ones who love you. We have found a nice place where you can live and it is only a short drive away from where Sarah and I will be, enabling us visitation on holidays and weekends. Wouldn't you like that, Mother? Sarah is looking forward to getting more acquainted with you. I think the two of you could—

A knock at the door stops Momma from continuing.

"Anna, it's them. Don't open it. It's them, I tell you," says Miss Janie, whispering, running up the stairs, pulling off her clothes as she goes.

"Mr. Pete?" Momma says, opening the door. There he stood in his three-piece suit and fancy Stetson hat. A woman in a white dress stood next to him. The dress was the whitest of white with not a single wrinkle; only the stripe of blue around her collar made the woman real at all.

"Anna? Girl, look at you. Don't tell me you've gone and gotten yourself knocked up again? My word. You coloreds are worse than rabbits," Mr. Pete says of my presence. "Well, Sarah and I are trying, but, you know, these things take time. It's nobody's fault, though. Not my fault, not her fault. No sir. Nobody's fault. I'm sure it'll happen soon. She's out in the car. She thought it would be best to not let Mother see her just yet. You know how things are. It's nobody's fault. It's just the way things are. Where is Mother?"

"She just went up the stairs. Mr. Pete?"

"What?"

"Well . . ."

"Spit it out, Anna. What's wrong?"

"Well, Miss Janie, she's been havin' visions again. She thinks there are people in the house. I don't think you're goin' to get her down here, if that's what you're aimin'."

"Well, that's why we hired this fine lady, Anna," says Mr. Pete, pushing Momma aside and walking over to the staircase. "Mother, it's me. Now, come on down."

"Petey? Is that my little Petey?" says Miss Janie, slowly coming down the stairs, then sitting on the third step from the top, peeking out from where the wall and staircase meet. She's taken off everything except her underclothes and plays with them as she speaks.

"Yes, Mother, it's your little . . . Petey."

"They're in the house, Petey. You have to protect me. They've come to get me. The devil sent them. You've got to protect me. They want to skin and boil me in the town square."

"That's why I'm here, Mother. I'm here to make sure you're safe and that no harm comes to you. So why don't you come down and this fine lady will help me get all the demons out of the house?"

"Really? You promise, Petey? Cross your heart and hope to die?" Miss Janie stands up and slowly begins to come down the stairs. "The devil isn't with you, is she?" says Miss Janie, stopping at the thought.

"No. There's no devil here. Now, come on." Miss

Janie doesn't move an inch. "Come on down. Mother!"

"Anna. Anna, look around and make sure that that devil isn't anywhere to be found."

"Mother, I've had enough of this nonsense! You are trying my patience. Don't make me have to come up there and get you. Now, stop this childishness and come down here this instant. And I mean right now!"

Miss Janie begins to cry and pulls off the rest of her clothes.

"Peter. Peter, my word! What in Christ's name is the delay? I want to be back in Atlanta by nightfall," says Miss Sarah, coming through the screen door.

The slam behind her triggers something in Miss Janie. Before, it was as if she thought the devil was in the house, but actually seeing her, in the flesh, makes her go to another place. All her visions seemed to gel into truth in that sighting. She sits on that step, frozen, peering through the railings like a prisoner, looking at Miss Sarah, whispering in fear. "I told you, Anna. I told you the devil was in the house. They've come to take me to the town square for public ridicule."

The woman in white walks up the stairs and starts to walk Miss Janie down, step by step. Each foot stops on each step, not daring to move to the next before its time. Miss Janie just stares, looking at Miss Sarah.

"Let me get her a blanket," says Momma, walking over to the cedar chest and pulling out her favorite. "She needs somethin' to cover her up."

"Thank you, Anna," says Mr. Pete.

"Peter, tell the girl we will no longer be needing her services. And tell her that the movers should be arriving tomorrow, so don't be tempted toward stealing anything. I know times are difficult for colored people, but they still have to work hard for what they get, just like the rest of us," says Miss Sarah, scanning the living room. "Of course, only a Nigra would dare want anything from this place."

"Yes, dear."

"Very good, then. Tell her, and let's go. We're behind schedule."

"Yes, dear. I'll be right out."

Miss Sarah storms out the same as when she came in. The door slams in Momma's face as she and the woman in white begin to walk Miss Janie to the car.

"Anna," says Miss Janie, as she's walking down the walk, "I told you. I told you."

"Yes, ma'am. You did. You sure did."

Once the woman in the white had settled Miss Janie in the back seat of the long beige Cadillac, Mr. Pete handed Momma some money and off they drove.

Momma had been taking care of someone else's "child," and now that child was gone—if not to the town square, then to a place that she'd be sure to hate just as much. Being lynched or boiled or even tarred and feathered was by no means a white worry, but Miss Janie's worry, broom and all, had swept her away, and the ridicule proved the same.

As Miss Janie feared, the devil came and took her away. We knew of a devil—in the form of Auntie Clariece, and before long, she, too, would appear.

After Momma locked up the Pattersons' house for what would be the last time, we started walking home. Momma pulled off her head scarf and her hair fell loose around her shoulders, framing her face. She had "white girl's" hair. That's what all the snotty-nosed children used to tell her when she was coming up. It used to make her cry, but now it didn't matter much. Gram had always told her to pay them no never-mind.

This time of year was always kind to Momma's skin. When the sun kissed her face, it made it like honey. But today, the clouds had rode in and they look as if at any moment they will break. Break they do, gradually at first; then, as the clouds meet, the downpour comes. Momma's pace refuses to alter. She keeps it steady, drifting along as if the rain doesn't exist.

Finally, we arrive at the front gate. We collapse. The money that Mr. Pete gave us is still in Momma's hand, but is soaked, except for where her tight grip has kept it dry. Junior runs from the porch and helps Momma to her feet. I feel like I'm being squeezed, then released. The movement is sharp.

It's abrupt. Quick breaths, then a big one. More short quick ones. I feel myself moving around. When Junior gets her to the porch, he sits her down in Poppa's rocker and tries to calm her, brushing her rain-drenched hair away from her tear-soaked face.

"Junior," says Leselle, standing at the screen door watching, "is Momma feeling the Spirit? Is she happy?"

<u>3</u>

... When I wash the dishes, I take off my wedding ring. I think of my momma. I think of Joseph and all the years we've been together. Then I think of you. I think of my boys and I think of this baby. That ring holds so many lives together. My hand feels naked when I don't have it on. . . .

J. T. is so strong. His strength is his weakness. I guess men are like that. The other night, I was in bed resting my eyes, because my nerves refuse me sleep. When he got in bed, I didn't budge; I just kept my eyes closed. I could feel his eyes looking at me. Ida Mae, he whispered, "I love you." I promise he did. I still didn't move. I wanted to roll over and let him know I knew, but I didn't. I know him too well. Still, you can only keep your eyes closed for so long. How I

wish he could say it without believing me
asleep . . .

"You should have seen him," said Anna, biting
her nails. "Boy, was he nervous."

"Girl, I can't even believe yo' momma let him up
in y'all house. Let alone give him the say-so to take
your hand," said Ida Mae, taking a swig from her
vodka bottle. "You wanna swallow? It's vodka—the
latest drink from up north."

"Chile, as much as you talk about up north,
you'd think you might as well move on up there. I
mean, if it's that great and all."

"I might do."

"Well, suit yourself, but I'm gonna be here and
I'm gonna to be Mrs. Joseph Henry Thomas. Sounds
nice, doesn't it?"

"It'll pro'bly sound better after another swiga this
here liquor," said Ida Mae, getting up and walking
around the kitchen. Corene, her mother, was at a
revival for the weekend, so it was just her and
Anna. "Have a drink. You 'bout to get married, so
you're old enough to have a drink without fear if
you wants one."

The bottle of vodka was on the kitchen table.
Anna poured herself a small drink.

"No, don't do that. I like to keep the top off till
we finish it or decide we finished," she said as

Anna reached to replace the top. *"It makes it more social that way. Open bottle, open heart. No one needs to feel like they can't reach for another drink if they wants one. That's what they mean by 'treat thy neighbor as thyself.' "*

"Quotin' the Bible, Ida Mae? That's not like you."

"Why not? Anybody can use the Bible to make their point. It's just a lotta the time, people don't like the point you tryin' to make."

"Well, cheers," said Anna, taking a sip.

"So, I know Cynthia didn't let Joe off easy."

"No. You know Momma wasn't goin' to just let him have me without having a li'l fun. Joe came and he was all dressed up. You could have cut a tomato clean with the crease on his britches. So Momma makes him sit there a long time before she even comes in the room to greet him. Then when she finally does come in the sittin' room, she acts like she doesn't know what it's about, and can't be bothered to pay mind to it. She says, 'You're Lucille's boy, correct?' and Joe says, 'Yessum.' Then Momma says, 'I'm sorry about her death. It's always hard on a child when they lose a mother. She was a good woman. Fine individual. Never heard a bad word spoken about her, and that's a rarity these days. I know she had it hard raising you when your father died.' So Joe is sittin' there fidgetin' and he says, 'Yessum,' like that's the only thing he knows.

So Momma never cracks a smile, and just looks at him and says, 'Well?' And I swear, J. T. was—"

"J. T.?" said Ida Mae, teasing Anna.

"That's my own li'l play name for him, you know. So I swear before God I thought J. T. was wettin' his britches and he says, 'Well, what?' And Momma says, 'Well, what, what?' And then, I swear, J. T. says, 'Oh, sorry, ma'am. Well, what, ma'am?' Because he thought Momma meant he should address her properly, but—"

"Anna, I gets it. Just go on with tellin' the damn story. Girla die of ol' age 'fore you finish tellin' it," said Ida Mae, filling up her and Anna's glasses.

"So, finally, J. T. gets it and then proceeds to ask for my hand. Well, Momma gets up from her chair and walks around the room real slowlike, then she stops at the window. And she says, 'Anna's father was killed when she was just a child. There's no need in rehashing the past, so I won't. But I had to raise her on my own, being both the mother and the father, just like your mother. It wasn't easy. I've tried to protect her as much as anyone could, but she's gettin' of age, and she seems to have taken a certain likin' to you. I'm still skeptical about you, but I knew your father from way back when. He seemed to be a good and decent man, so I can only hope and pray you'll grow up to be the same.'

"Momma said all that still facin' the window, as

*if admiring the roses in the front-yard flower bed. I
could see J. T. from the crack in the door. He was
takin' deep swallows like he had the cotton mouth.
Then Momma turned around and looked right at
him and she says, 'Were the situation different and
Anna's father still alive, you wouldn't even have to
be talkin' to me. I know that makes you feel some-
what uncomfortable. Mothers rarely get to make
any decision for their children. But I love Anna with
all my life and it isn't easy to give her over. Will
you make her happy?' Then J. T. swallowed real
hard and says, 'I'll try.' And then Momma says—
and Ida Mae you should've heard—she says, 'See
that you do,' and she walked out the room without
another word said. She almost knocked my head
off when she opened the door. I know she knew I
was listenin'. I ran in and gave J. T. some ice water
and we hugged, but he wouldn't kiss me because
he was afraid Momma was goin' to come back in.
So! What do you think about that?"*

*"What I think? Well, I think it calls for another
drank," said Ida Mae, grabbing the vodka bottle off
the table.*

"Will you be my first maid?"

*"Girl, what kind of foolishness you talking?" said
Ida Mae, prancing over to Anna, a smile flowing
freely. "You know not to be askin' me nothin' like*

*that. Of course I'm gonna be your first maid, fool.
But don't 'spect me to wear white."*

Junior finally got Momma to stop crying. It wasn't
the Spirit that made her cry. No. Not this time. He
made Leselle and Edward stay in the house until
the sobs refused to fall. Leo and Leon stayed silent.
Leo brought a face cloth to cool her; and Leon, a
drink of ice water. I began to feel comfortable again
as my surroundings at least settled, if not became
normal.

"I need to stop this nonsense and get some food
cooked and on the table," said Momma, getting up
from Poppa's rocker and going through the screen
door. "Your Poppa'll be home soon."

"Don't worry 'bout that, Momma. He and Teacake
went over to the Nail after work. They ain't gonna
be home for a spell," said Junior.

"That's not like him to go to no juke joint on a
Monday when he's got work in the mornin'."
Momma was looking at Junior, but no explanation
came. So Momma kept on, vocalizing what her
questioning eyes couldn't say. "Junior? Junior, what
is it?"

"They got these new machines in down at the
mill. Word had been passed 'round that when these
here machines came, some men was gonna be laid
off. That was a whiles back, so nobody thought too
much about it. Ever'body thought it was just talk in

the wind so we'd work harder. Well, this mornin' when we got to work, the boss man called ever'-body 'round to the front of the mill, then he called out the names of the people who was gonna be laid off." Junior didn't look at Momma. He slowly swung his left foot around, rotating it back and forth like he was moving something on the floor, but nothing was there. "The boss man said that they would be paid for another week's work, but that there was no need in them staying on for that week and that they could pick up they money and leave."

"He called out the names in front of ever'body?" said Momma, coming closer to Junior, propping herself on the table, using its legs to keep her balance as her own began to fail her.

"The boss man said he was sorry and he wished there was an easier way, but that this was the 'quickest and most efficient' way to handle this 'development.' "

"And what did your Poppa do when he called out y'all's names?" said Momma, trying to prepare herself for anything Poppa might bring back with him from the juke joint.

"That's the thing, Momma. He didn't call out our names."

"Then what are you talkin' about, Junior?" said Momma, aggravation coating her tongue. I had never heard that tone from her before.

"I mean they called out only his name . . ."

"Oh, Lord . . ."

"I heard Poppa's name called and I just—"

"Oh, Lord . . ."

"—knowed that my name was next. But the next name came up, then the next, and my name wahn't on the list. I even went up and looked at the list after, but my name wahn't on it," said Junior, raising his voice to make Momma hear what happened, to explain it, make her understand.

Momma slid down the back of the chair till the seat stopped her fall. Junior went behind her and started rubbing her shoulders. He told Momma that one of the boss man's boys told him he got to keep his job because he was young and could read. He was also told they thought that in the long run, he'd be able to run the machines and take the mill, which they were now going to start calling "a plant," into the "twentieth century," and it was "past due." Some fifty-odd years past due, but I'm told Mississippi has had a record of being behind.

Junior said Poppa was too much of a man to show he was hurting. So he just took his money and he, Teacake, and a bunch of the other men went down to the Nail to swallow their sorrows behind false laughter and watered-down corn liquor.

For a moment, Momma had forgotten about the trials of her day. Forgotten that the devil came and took Miss Janie away. Forgotten she, too, had no job of which to speak. But when it hit her, it hit like a punch to the stomach and the lack of wind that follows. She didn't know how she was going to tell Poppa about Miss Janie. The money Mr. Pete gave her was a generous amount, but it wouldn't last forever. They had always depended on Poppa's and Junior's earnings to get us through, but now, Junior was the only one with a wage.

For the first time, I could feel that Momma had forgotten about me. She didn't rub me or make reference to me once. No hum telling me everything was going to be all right. She wasn't able to deal with what was still months away when right now needed all the strength her swollen heart and ankles could muster. And as my brothers do when Poppa is in a mood, I sat still, hoping I, too, would continue to go unnoticed.

"You all stop playin' in that tub and come eat. The food's gettin' cold," says Momma to Edward and Leselle. The two of them always take a bath together because Leo and Leon would only take a bath with each other. Edward and Leselle came in and sat at the table, joining Junior, Leo, and Leon.

"We ain't gonna wait on Poppa?" says Edward.

"No. We're going to eat tonight without him. Poppa'll eat later on, when he comes in," says Momma, with steady delivery. "Junior, will you say grace, please?"

Junior looks up from his plate with surprise. Rarely did grace get said out loud at the table. Poppa wouldn't allow it.

"Lord. Bless this bounty which we are 'bout to

receive and look over this family in its wakin' hour. Thine is the kingdom, the . . ."

Singing starts coming in from outside. It's Poppa. You can tell it's a song he carried from the juke joint, the only place where the blues can be sung with a smile.

"Leo, Leon, Edward, Leselle, go on in your room. We'll eat in a minute."

"But . . ."

"Edward, please, now. I don't have time to go back and forth with you. Now, please, baby, just do as I say."

They go to the room. Momma and Junior go to the screen door, and sure enough, there is Poppa singing in full voice. Teacake is holding him up. Junior starts to run out and help, feeling he should, but Momma holds him back.

"I've brought you a present," says Teacake. "He was sangin' louder den the gal at the Nail, so dey kicked his ass out, told him to go on home. In all my days, I ain't nevah seen 'em tell a payin' customah to go home. Joe, boy, you know you sho showed out!"

"Dat's right! Told me. Told Joseph Henry Thomas to take it on home. Dat his money weren't no good!" says Poppa, walking up the porch steps with Teacake's help.

This is a switch for Teacake. Usually *he's* the town clown. Always grinning to get his way and having a fun time along the way. So much so that eyes no longer raised with his passing. They say he was called Teacake because he was too small and didn't quite rise enough to be a biscuit. It was surprising to see big ol' Poppa draped over his little body. No one would believe he'd have the strength to carry him. I'm sure it put a strain on his wooden leg, a leg made and donated from the very lumber mill that took his real one away.

"Well, looky here," says Poppa, looking up at Junior and Momma—and me. "Greetin' me at the door. Ain't that some nice? Sweet as pie." Poppa laughs as if he'd made a joke, but the humor is lost on the others. Teacake helps him through the screen door. Junior keeps wanting to lend a hand, but Momma keeps a strong grip on his arm, so much so that the tips of her fingers whiten.

"Well, smell right nice in here. And looka there, Teacake; the supper table all made up and ready for me. See there. That's right nice. That's the way it's s'posed to be. Y'all musta heard me comin' and set the table up nicely. Where the rest of the boys? Leselle! Leo! Y'all get ya asses out here! Edward! And what's that other li'l nigga's name? Get on out here! We gonna eat. Poppa's home! I'm gonna sit at the head of my table wit my family and we gonna eat. Get on out here, now!"

Momma runs over to Poppa and the smell of liquor makes me squirm. "J. T., let them be. We was just gettin' ready to have some supper. We heard ya coming and set the table right nice for you," says

Momma, placing herself under Poppa's free arm. They walk him to the kitchen table. Junior just stands there, watching.

"Den let's eat, den. Didn't I tell you li'l niggas to get on out here?! Ya Poppa home!" says Poppa, staggering to stand. Junior moves toward him, but Momma gives him a look that stops him. A look from Poppa may make you step forward or even step back, but only a mother's gaze can stop you still. "Listen, now. When I says somethin' 'round here, I means for it to be done. Y'all movin' 'round slower'n a gran'momma on a rainy day."

"I'll get them, J. T. Just hold on a minute. I'll get 'em. Junior, get a plate out for your Poppa and Tea-cake. Teacake, have some supper?" says Momma, going toward the boys' bedroom.

"So, I sees how it is," says Poppa. "I sees how it is. That's it, huh. I guess Junior runnin' thangs 'round here now. Is that it? He got his plate up there at the head of the table and now he gotta pull out a plate for me at my own damn supper table. Is that it? That's how it is, huh?"

"No, Poppa, I . . ."

"Watch what you say, boy," says Poppa, getting up from the table and looking at the settings. "So you think you the man of the house now? You the big nigga on this side of the tracks, huh?" Junior doesn't answer. "Boy, don't you hear me askin' you a question? Answer me!"

Poppa takes one of those hands that make the

newspaper look small and grabs Junior by the shirt. With the other, he grips his face, molding it like Momma would the dough for biscuits. "You think you the man of the house now? Huh, boy? So what you gonna do now? You gonna go run and get yo' Bible now? What the Lawd gonna do for ya now? 'Cuz I sho don't see Him around. The Lawd is funny that way, ain't He?"

Poppa pushes Junior out of the kitchen and through the living room. Junior falls to the floor. Leselle and Edward stand behind me and Momma while Leo and Leon stand in front of us, watching Poppa's every move.

I start feeling . . . feeling pressure, like the walls are closing in on me. I . . . I . . . there's noise. It's pounding, pounding real fast, and . . . and I can feel things rushing up past me, real fastlike. Momma starts breathing really heavylike and I hear Leo and Leon scream together, "Momma!" There is a release from around me, then nothing.

Black.

In the living room, on the end table next to the couch, is a ceramic elephant that Missus Anderson gave to Anna—and Joseph—on her wedding day. When Anna was coming up, there were always elephants in the house. Missus Anderson collected them. When people had to buy her a gift and couldn't think of what to bring, it was a safe bet that she would be pleased as punch to get an elephant. She had all sizes in her collection, so much so that there would be several in one spot—an elephant family.

Missus Anderson believed that elephants were wise. It's said that their memory is magical even though they appear slow. Though huge beasts as they are, they are gentle when it comes to taking care of their own.

The one she gave Anna—and Joseph—was gray with pink on the insides of its ears. Its trunk was at attention. Anna oftentimes rearranged the furnishings with the seasons, but the elephant was always in the same place: on the end table facing the door at the front of the house. Sometimes when Anna was nervous, she'd rub the elephant like one would pet a pet that was a part of the household, stroking it between its ears, along its back.

"This is one of my first elephants," said Missus Anderson. "Your father gave it to me shortly after we started courting. He knew how to win my favor, but even more, knew how to keep it.

"It was the sweetest thing. He'd been away on 'family business,' and when he came back, he said that he brought something back for me. But—before he'd give it to me, he wanted to know if I had 'something' for him. What he meant by that something was a wooden nickel. A kiss. Just like men.

Always wanting something before they give what it is they have for you. Of course, I didn't need a reason to give him a kiss. We were always neckin' every chance we could."

Anna covered the grin on her face at the thought of her mother ever neckin', and her actually admitting to it. Even on this, her wedding day, Missus Anderson had never once said anything about the facts of life to Anna. Some things just are never talked about.

"I suppose they still use that term? Neckin'? When you get older, you tend to lose sight of the latest sayings. But I gave your father a kiss that he wouldn't soon forget. Then I immediately asked for my present. 'Close your eyes,' he said. I did for a moment, then when he turned around to get it out of his bag, I opened my eyes a bit and watched him. 'Are they closed?' he said. I said that they were, to just hurry up. I watched him bend down, because I liked to see him bend, and he pulled out a box. He asked me again if they were 'still closed.' Then I did close them for real. He walked back over and handed me the box.

"Though I wanted to rip it open, being the lady that I am, I unpeeled each piece of tape as not to damage the wrapping paper, so I could use it again come Christmas. When that was done, I folded the paper, oh, so carefully that he seemed to be more *excited than I. When I opened the box, under a bed of straw was this elephant. I thought it was so sweet. He could have brought back anything, a ring, flowers, anything, and I would have been satisfied, but it took a sweetheart to bring me that elephant to add to my then small collection."*

Missus Anderson loved to reminisce about her husband. It wasn't a sad thing for her. It brought her joy. There was so much Anna didn't know about her father. Even though the money seemed to have been around when she was a child, she never knew what made it so. Or why or how he died. There always seem to be some things children never know about their parents, and as a child, it doesn't seem important, for it isn't in our reality. It's not until you get older that you realize how much, and how little, you really know about anything.

Missus Anderson was smart and read what seemed like a book a day. Books set her mind at ease, taking her to faraway lands, lands that her feet would never grace. Many times she was accused of being "cidity," because she kept to herself. Sometimes people are accused of being cidity not because they feel they're better than everybody, but because they feel they're different. And it's a difference that can make people feel alone, even in a crowd.

As bright as Missus Anderson was, she was as much superstitious. There were unwritten rules in her

house. No sweeping while people were in the room.
If you touch someone's feet with the broom, it's bad
luck. "That's why when people get married they jump
over the broom." You also couldn't whistle in the
house, for it was said to wake bad spirits. But above
all, she believed in the power of the elephants.

"The reason I keep elephants around is because
they bring good luck. I'm giving this one to you to
watch over your house. If you point the trunk
toward the door, it will protect you like elephants
in Africa do their young. It will bring safety to you
and yours to come, and that is all I can ever wish
for you, my daughter."

... There's that day when you wake up and
see your child is no longer a child. And even
though it has been going on before your eyes,
you wonder when it happened. What moment?
What second? But you can't put your finger on
it. I don't want to hang on too long, but I don't
want to let go too soon . . .

"Momma. Momma." It's Junior. I recognize his
voice. "Wake up, Momma."
Leo is putting a rag on Momma's face. I feel better, but boiling. The pounding around me is steady
again. Momma is on the floor. Leon tells Momma
to wake up. He fans her with the Mahalia Jackson

hand fan, distributed by Turner's Funeral Home, trying to cool her off.

"He's dead," says Edward.

"Hush up, Ed. He ain't dead, he's just drunk," says Junior.

"Leave him be. Get away from him," says Momma, coming to.

"It's awright, Momma. It's Junior."

"He's dead. You killed him, Junior," screams Edward.

"Hush up, before I kill you," screams Junior. "He's just drunk, Momma. He's sleepin' it off."

"Junior, what happened to you? Did he . . ."

"Shhh, Momma. Shhh. I'm fine. You passed out." Momma tries to get up. The heavy pounding starts again, but Junior tells her to stay put for a while. She rests her head back on the pillow some-one had placed under us while she was out.

"We thought you were dead," says Leo. "You started to fall and me and Leon caught you."

"That's my boys. That's my li'l babies." Momma feels her stomach and slowly runs her hands all the way down under me. She looks at her hand.

"You're bleedin', Momma!" says Leo.

"It's all right, baby. Momma's fine. Junior? Junior, get me a wet washcloth." Junior gets up and goes to the bathroom. "Don't worry, li'l Lisa. Don't you worry about a thing. Momma's gonna take good care of you. Nothin's gonna hurt you. Nothin's gonna hurt any of you. I promise. Mark my word."

4

... It's funny, though both the moon and the sun shine down on me, the feeling is something all together different.

Not so much on my skin, but within. It's like the light that makes me see through the darkness, making me know it's not all bad. It sounds silly, I know. But if nothing else, I'm feeling a lot these days—whether the kick of this child or the pain I feel when thinking of losing her . . .

It's been five weeks since Poppa got laid off. Junior's black eye is almost healed, changing in shape from half- to crescent moon. Momma made him rub a tablespoon on it every day to get the blood circulating again, "a trick I got from Ida Mae, who did it to remove hickies from her neck."

Everybody at work knew where Junior "caught" his black eye, so they didn't bother to ask. They knew he'd catch hell from Poppa about being kept on even though Poppa pretended it didn't bother him. "Ol' man's s'posed to rest and let his chilren take care of him." They knew Poppa was just talking the talk. Twenty-some years is a long time to know a man.

Poppa grew up working in that mill, as did so many others, but now, it was over. No more sounds of lumber hitting the table or sawdust underfoot. No more splinters working themselves out of skin unaware of their presence. All of that was over, opening its way toward other things, though no one knew what.

Junior just goes to work, then comes directly home, trying to make his absence and appearance as nonthreatening as possible. Words rarely came out of Junior's mouth. He knows no matter what you say or what your intentions, at times, people only hear what they want to hear, leaving little leeway for change.

Since he was laid off, Poppa has had nothing to do and all day to do it in. He's been hanging out with Teacake most of the time, going down to the Rusty Nail, drinking like there's no tomorrow, and from where his barstool sat, that probably seems true. Sometimes he gets so drunk he falls asleep out in the yard. Junior asks Momma if she wants him to go fetch him and bring him into the house, but

Momma says to just let him be, to let him sleep it off out there. "Sleeping under the stars can do a proud man good," she says.

The news of Miss Janie being taken away by "the devil" seems like a small thing compared to that night that Momma passed out, and the fight and all that surrounded it.

It really looked bad for Junior. Poppa was drunk and wasn't budging much. Junior got in a couple of good blows before Poppa caught him dead square in the eye. The whole time, Poppa was just laughing and swaggering, swaggering like his rocking chair right before a twister. He kept telling Junior, "If you throws a punch, you better make sure you means it!" And without question, you could tell that Junior did. Teacake left when the first lick was thrown. He knew Poppa could have taken a swing at him if he got in the way. When you're drunk, everyone can look either like your worst enemy or your best friend. Teacake didn't want to risk which one he might be on that given night.

The next morning came as usual. The rooster crowed. The sun rose. I don't know why I thought it wouldn't, but it did, and it was as if nothing had happened. Yesterday became yesterday as today became today. You could even hear the birds singing. I imagine they sang right often, doing their dances around the birches, but not always could they be heard from our wooden frame house.

Poppa slept late that day, and Junior had already

gone off to work before he found his way out of bed. Poppa didn't even see Junior's eye till that night, when all he said was if he had a mind to, he'd give him another to match.

"If you had a mind?" said Junior, and he went to wash up for supper.

Poppa pretended like he didn't hear him, but I believe he did. He wasn't fully recovered from the corn liquor that stole the water from his body, so the space between his ears was filled with other things besides Junior's words. His groans and the wrinkles about his forehead were proof of that.

When Momma told Poppa the news about Miss Janie, she thought he'd be fit to be tied. She counted to ten, tapping out each number with her fingertips on me as she did. Then Momma placed herself firmly between the chair, the table, and Poppa.

"J. T.?" Momma said, almost like she wished she hadn't even started it, but now it was done and she had to go on with it. "Yesterday . . . see, while I was at Miss Janie's . . . now, don't go gettin' yourself all upset. But . . . see, Mr. Pete came. You remember me talkin' about Mr. Pete, Miss Janie's son . . . ?"

"What you carryin' on 'bout dem crackers for first thang in the mornin' when I'm tryin' to enjoy my meal?" said Poppa, dropping his knife and fork on the table. "You tryin' to put a bad taste in my mouth?"

"No, J. T. No. It's just that . . . well, you see, they come yesterday, Mr. Pete and his wife, and they took Miss Janie, so . . ."—Momma took a deep breath, so big I moved way down low—". . . they said that they wouldn't be needin' me anymore. That they would look after her from here on end."

Poppa sucked on his teeth, making a noise that sent a chill up Momma's back—a back that needed nothing else added, for I was providing plenty. Then he picked up his knife and fork and started eating again. He didn't say anything. It was like he was trying to decide what to say. Momma just stood there and the beat of my heart filled her ears, and even the words she spoke, she couldn't hear.

"I asked around to see if anybody knew of anybody that might need some help . . ."

"No need in doin' that. Your job gonna be to look after me," said Poppa as if he was hiding the fact that he was pleased with what he heard. "I can't have you runnin' 'round waitin' on dem crackers when there's me to take care of now. Yo' mammy would be tickled pink to know that her li'l girl weren't workin' for nobody no more. Mo' biscuits."

Momma put three more biscuits on his plate. Without looking up, he began to eat them, sucking his teeth as he ate. The sound made Momma shiver.

Momma tells me I was fertilized on Halloween. She'd tease me about it, but say I didn't have to worry about any bad spirits, for they always passed over the innocent. Poppa, she said, was in a good mood that night. They were home alone, as my brothers were at the Halloween carnival thrown by Mr. Jefferson in his barn every year for the community's colored children. Mr. Jefferson was a rich old white man, but he chose to live on the colored side of town. He wasn't "showy rich," so to look at him, you'd never know, which gave all the white folks that knew plenty to talk about. They thought he was "sick in the noggin," which is fine, "when you can afford to be." Most of the colored people thought he was crazy, too, but they never failed to show up for his carnival every year. "Always nice to step on a white man's property and not have to work."

Junior took the boys, even though he really didn't want to. He'd gotten to the point where he felt he was too old to be seen at functions that were for children. Momma told him that he was going as a grown-up, a "chaperon," and not as a child. That changed his thinking, as only words from a mother can.

Momma said Poppa was being real sweetlike. "Romantic." An uncle had passed, his last kin except for Clariece, and left him some money, which came in the mail that day. He gave all the boys a quarter to take to the carnival with them, which took them all for a loop. It was nothing compared to those folded bills from Gram, but nonetheless, a quarter—in Mississippi, in a young boy's hands—meant something special. Momma said the boys were so shocked that they thought it was a trick instead of a treat.

With leftover fabric she'd gotten from Miss Janie, she made herself a dress and was looking right nice, "if I dare say so myself."

"Your Poppa was so sweet that night. It reminded me of why I fell in love with him," Momma said to me long before she ever told Poppa there even was a me. "He's a good man, your Poppa. Deep down, he is good. It's just the deeper the treasure, the longer you have to dig before the wealth can be enjoyed. And you'll be his li'l girl and he's gonna spoil you rotten. You'll see. That's what's wrong. There's just too many smelly, rotten boys runnin' around here. He needs a girl around him to find that soft spot in his heart that I know is there."

The day she was telling me this story was the day she decided my name would be Lisa. She said Gram had a sister named Lisa that passed away shortly after birth, and she thought Lisa would be a nice tribute.

As my story goes, the moon was full that Halloween night. When Momma walked the boys out to the porch to see them off, there it was, in all its glory, shining down on Momma in her new dress. Her hair was down around her shoulders, and she said it glistened in the night. With the scraps left over from the dress, she had made a matching ribbon for her hair, but ended up tying it around her neck. She said it made her look like a princess.

Momma said she looked up to the moon, peeking over the fields, and there sitting next to it was a star, the first star of the night—the wishing star.

"As the boys walked out of the yard, I looked at that big moon. They say it's made of cheese, but I know it's made of dreams," said Momma, taking eggs from the chicken house, telling the story as if it happened the day before. "And I saw it. It had just appeared when I looked up, like it was waitin' on me to come outside before comin' to call. The wishin' star. And I smiled and I looked up and I closed my eyes. Made a wish. Do you know what I wished for, li'l Lisa? I wished for you. As much as I knew your Poppa was against it, I still did it. And when I opened my eyes, that wishin' star winked at me. I'm most sure of it. Kind of like it was tellin' me to open my eyes and see my wish come true."

Momma said shortly after the stars lit the way, Poppa joined her on the porch. He had shaved and was as handsome as the first day she laid eyes on him, bowlegs and all. Funny what money in an empty pocket can do for the spirit. Poppa rarely had the comfort of choice.

That entire evening was a good one, filled with what would be fond memories. When the boys got back, they had turned their quarters into much more. Between the two of them, Edward and Leselle had closed down the cake and pie walk; Leo and Leon had gotten together and guessed how many beans were in a jar, winning a dollar. Momma said

I couldn't have wished for a better night to be fertilized, and about that, I took her word. It was a good night, she said, a good night for all. The seed had been planted.

... At the market today, I heard news that Miss Janie died, just two days after they took her away. Everybody knows what's best for everybody else. Different things get taken from you in the course of a life. The space between young and old is as far as Detroit is from Mississippi.

Of course there are stories floating 'round about you. You know how people like to talk just to hear themselves talk. They always say it in earshot of me. I just smile and say, "Oh, really?" They hate that. You'd be so proud. I just wish I would hear of you from you. No one makes me laugh like you, and how I could use a good laugh now. I wish I could write something funny on these pages, but . . .

"Girl, Missus Anderson is gonna have a fit when she find out," said Ida Mae, examining the produce at the market, scoping for bruises passed off as quality.

"Well, who's gonna tell her?" said Anna. "Besides, it's just a job around the woman's house. She seems nice enough. Her chilren near grown and it ain't gonna be no hassle. It'll give us a li'l extra money to bring into the house."

"*What you think of this material here? It look nice with my skin color, don'tcha think?*" said Ida Mae, holding up a purple floral print and putting it next to her skin.

"*That fabric goes up against white folks' skin, girl, white folks who intend to buy it. So if you don't intend to buy, then I suggest that you put it down as you found it,*" said the store clerk.

"*Do you see this?*" said Ida Mae, pulling out a wad of money with a big rubber band wrapped around it. "*This! is money! Cash dollar bills. You know what we do with money? We go in stores and buys things, and that keeps you in business, and . . .*"

"*Ida Mae,*" said Anna, taking Ida Mae by the hand and pushing her toward the door of the store.

"*. . . if we didn't, you wouldn't even have this here li'l ol' pitiful place you calls a store!*"

"*Are you crazy? You gonna get the both of us strung up, and I still didn't get what I came for,*" said Anna once she got Ida Mae outside and out of shouting distance of the store clerk.

"*We don't have to take that kind of mess from him. That's what's wrong with colored people down here. Too damn 'fraid to raise they voices. Hell, I was just lookin' at the material. Wahn't like I was spittin' on it. He needs colored folks to look at it, 'cuz can't none of 'em white women pull off wearin'*

'em colors. So all it's gonna do is sit there gettin'
ate up by moths anyway."

"Eaten, *Ida Mae.* And it may do just that, but
that's no reason for you to go spoutin' off like that.
You're goin' to get us in trouble."

"Have I ever got you in trouble before?" Anna
looks at Ida Mae. "Scratch that question. 'Sides,
yo' concern oughta be how Missus Anderson gonna
shoot that dirty dog of yourn when she find out he
made you get a job."

"First off, missy ma'am," said Anna, stopping
and putting her hands on her hips, "he did not
make me get a job. I got a job on my own because I
wanted to do somethin'. Unlike many, my husband
doesn't make *me* do anythin'. I do as I please."

"Well, well, well. Ain't yo' panties pink with
flowers on 'em! All I know is I can hear Cynthia
now, sayin' that no chile of hers needs to be slavin'
in no white woman's kitchen. I suggest you tell her
'fore she hear it in the wind."

"I'll tell Momma when I see her, but right now,
I've got to get home and figure out what I'm going
to cook, bein' as you got us run out of the
market."

Anna and Ida Mae walked for a spell till they got
to the house. Joseph was still at work, and they sat
giggling like they were at the creek and young
again. Anna was so pleased to be married, and to

the man that she had wanted so. Constantly all smiles back then.

When the time was right and Ida Mae thought Anna was in the proper mood, she finally asked what had been itching her since the reception at the house after the wedding.

"Spill the beans," said Ida Mae. "Come on. Tell it."

"Tell what?"

"How was the honeymoon?"

"Ida Mae, you know we didn't go nowhere. We stayed here. You know Joe couldn't get the time off work. You just can't let it rest, can you?"

"Girl, I'm not talkin' 'bout where you went. I'm talkin' 'bout what you did! Now, if you wanna tell me where y'all did it, I'm open to that, too."

"Ida Mae!" said Anna with a scream, but blushing all the same.

"Ooh! Looky you. It musta been good. You turnin' all red and lightin' up just like one of those white chilren," said Ida Mae, with a grin from ear to ear.

Anna did turn red, but this time, it wasn't due to blushing. She stood up.

"Don't you ever say that to me, Ida Mae. If you call yourself my friend, then don't do me like that."

Anna walked from the kitchen and went out to the swing on the porch. Ida Mae sat at the table for a few seconds more, then got up, walked over, and stood at the screen door, looking through tiny holes in search for her next words.

"Anna? Precious, you awright?" Anna didn't answer; she just shrugged her shoulders. From where Ida Mae was standing, that could have meant yes or no. Ida Mae came outside and started to walk toward the swing. "Anna, I'm so sorry. Precious, you know I didn't mean it like that. You know I love you wit all my heart, and I would kill anythang that hurt a hair on your body. You know I didn't mean to hurt you. I was just havin' girl talk, that's all. Just girl talk."

Anna began crying stale tears. Ida Mae sat next to her on the swing. With her arms, she held Anna and with the leg that could still reach the porch, she pushed off to set the swing in motion.

"Go on, precious, let it all out. That's right, just let it all out. Ida Mae is here. Let it out."

The steady grinding and popping sound of the chain hooked up from the ceiling to the armhandle of the swing served as a distraction. They sat there rocking, so neither of them noticed Joseph coming up the walk.

"Anna? Anna, what's wrong?"

"Nothing, J. T.," said Anna, wiping the tears from her eyes and attempting laughter. "Me and Ida Mae

just talkin' about ol' times. I was tickled, that's all. Just tickled.''

"Yeah, thinkin' back to when—''

Joseph cut Ida Mae off.

"I didn't ask you nothin', Ida Mae. Well, it don't look to me like you 'just tickled.' I know whatevah it is has somethin' to do with your foolishness, Ida Mae. I ain't gonna have you comin' ovah to my house, puttin' ideas in Anna's head and gettin' her all worked up. She my wife now, not one of your li'l play girlfriends.''

"Listen here, Mister Joseph Henry Thomas. I have known Anna longer—!''

Anna grabbed her arm and Ida Mae quieted.

"J. T., it was nothin'. Nothin'. Just let it be. Please.''

Joseph walked through the screen door, letting it slam behind him. Anna and Ida Mae stood there on the porch looking at each other, and the swing still moved back and forth, though no one sat there to enjoy its comfort.

"I'll talk to you later,'' said Anna. She walked to the screen door and opened it. "Go on now. I'll talk to you later.'' She slid her hand along the screen till it met with where the wood flushed against the door. It didn't make a sound. Anna then disappeared into the house where her honeymoon had taken place.

"Yes. Yes, precious, you sure will."

That was the day Joseph decided he didn't want Ida Mae on his property. Anna and Ida Mae still snuck sometimes. Besides, it wasn't Joseph's property. It was Missus Anderson's. But Ida Mae wasn't her favorite person, either. Or so it seemed.

Two pieces of news came today—one by mail, and Poppa's mouth serving as messenger for the other.

First the good, which often is overlooked without a thought, for the bad always seems to steal focus. The news by mail turned out to be a letter from Ida Mae, postmarked Chicago. Momma took the letter and went to the bathroom. She hooked the door and, with that done, took a deep breath. She knew being in the bathroom wouldn't draw much attention should Poppa walk in. We had been spending lots of time in there lately. Momma says I always keep her on her toes and her backside. In a way, I was pleased. Momma seldom took a moment to sit down. Stillness never comes easy.

Once we were safely locked and comfortable, she looked at the envelope for a long time, examining her name and address and every mark on it. She hugged it. She knew it could only be from one person. With a careful hand, she opened it, not wanting to make any unnecessary wrinkle on the paper that held words she'd waited to read.

Dearest Precious Anna:

How is that no-good husband of yourn (smile)? Enough about him. I know it's been a spell since you heard from me, but thangs move so fast up here I barely have time to piss in the pot, let alone write a letter. You know I likes to talk more than write (smile). But I had some free time, so here it is.

The reason I have time is I had to quit my last job. It was in this woman's house. I should have knowed it wasn't gonna work out. The first day, she said, "Coffee," and I said, "Yes, milk and sugar." It was downhill from there.

Believe it or not, the old bag really wanted me to clean. She kept saying "gal this" and "gal that." She gal-ed me one time too many, so I went in the kitchen, pulled out ever'thang she had in the 'fridgerator, a fancy name for icebox, and cooked me a nice lunch. I left a big mess like nobody's bizness. When she told me I was fired, I knew it was time for me to go. You know how I gets. I mean, get (smile).

There is plenty 'a colored folk up here, but the white people just as downright mean, pro'bly meaner than the ones down South. These here crackers are just slicker is all.

I hope that bowlegged fool of yourn is treatin' you right. I'll take a hot comb to his ass if he ain't. And Joseph Thomas, if you readin' this here letter, so help me, I'll put somethin' real good on you—and you know I'm just wild enough to do it.

Well, my precious, I gotta go for now, but I'll write again soon.
Love always,
Ida Mae

The letter came as such a big surprise, every tooth in Momma's mouth showed. She hadn't seen Ida Mae since right before the twins were born. Ida Mae knew nothing of me, so Momma began to think about how shocked she would be when she heard the news.

Throughout their youth, Ida Mae had always talked about making her way up north, and finally she did. She had written Momma a few times since, but there was never a return address. Ida Mae never seemed to settle in one place for too long a time, always in search of the latest thing.

The letter put Momma in good spirits, which meant that that goodness, like the nourishment the roots of a tree provide for leaves years away, was passed on to me.

. . . You can let something go, but that doesn't mean it goes away. News comes in many ways. Whether it's a letter or a postcard from you or just a memory, it's something I can truly say is mine.

When J. T. isn't here, the boys and I sit around

reading books. When we've gone through them all, the boys make up the funniest stories. I sit there listening, as their minds run wild, until I slip into my own fantasy world.

When they reach the end of their tale, I say how wonderful it is, then they begin another, while mine remains the same. There's no risk involved in a fantasy . . .

That brings us to the second bit of news, this news coming not from post, but Poppa.

As I said earlier, I was growing at a steady rate and it wouldn't be long now before I'd do more than just show; I would be making my appearance, as that wishing star had done many months ago. Being so, Poppa made Momma forget about Ida Mae's letter without his even knowing it existed.

"James and Clariece gonna be stoppin' in on us tomorrow. James is preaching a revival down in Haightville and gonna stop by this way to see you. Clariece thought it'd be a good idea to pay a visit," said Poppa, mashing the yellow of his over-easy eggs until they ran runny. "Won't be long 'fo' they chile is due, and I think it'll do Clariece some good to spend some time witchu."

Poppa said this like he was a machine, like a machine that had replaced the real thing. There was no air getting to me. Momma had stopped breathing, but just for a few breaths. Poppa took a piece of light bread and stirred up the yolk till the bread,

soaked, became limp. Then he folded it in two and
put it into his mouth, seeming to swallow without
a single chew. Momma, too, became limp and with
his words, she might as well have been the light
bread swallowed whole, for any sense of form, me
or otherwise, seemed to disappear.

Junior looked at Momma. He knew what was
going on. Momma didn't tell him, she didn't tell
anyone, but he knew something was happening.
Whether it was voiced or not didn't change matters.
He and I were the only one of the children that
knew what Poppa was talking about, or the only
ones that let on to knowing.

"Well, Joe, I wish you'd've told me sooner. Goodness. There's lots I need to do around here to make
the place presentable," Momma said finally, finding
the words that she felt should come out even
though their meaning served as nothing to her other
than something to hold on to in a moment of
instability.

"Don't worry, Momma, I'll help you 'round
here," said Junior, getting up, clearing his plate
from the table. Leo and Leon followed his lead. Edward and Leselle sat there watching Poppa, doing
to their eggs as he was doing to his. To them, it
looked like he was playing with his food, which
was not allowed.

"No, Junior. I told Teacake you'd go over wit me
to his place and help him out. One of his cows is
'specting a calf and he gonna need some help," said

Poppa, his mouth full, the sound of the sopping bread smacking behind ever' word.

"But, Poppa, Momma needs—"

"Boy, you smellin' yo'self again? I said we gonna go over to Teacake's and help him out. Now, he's a friend of mine. He been like a uncle to you and you can't take some of your precious time to help him out?"

When Momma heard the word *precious,* I felt a jolt of lightning run through her. It again reminded her of Ida Mae's letter and how she wanted to read it without having to go to the bathroom for privacy.

"Go on with your Poppa. I'll be fine. The boys'll be around if I need them."

"Not me," screamed Edward.

"Me neither," Leselle said, following Edward's lead. "I want to see that cow have a baby. I didn't even know a cow had no belly button."

"That's my boys," said Poppa, getting up from the table, Leselle and Edward following close behind. "The twins will stay here witchu. Keep you company."

"See there, Leselle, you just wanted to go 'cuz I said I was goin'."

"No, I ain't."

"Yeah, you is."

"Both of you just hush."

"You ain't the boss of us, Junior," said Edward.

"Sho ain't," said Leselle.

Junior turned and looked at Momma, then went

out the screen door last, catching it before it slammed. Leo and Leon got up from the table. Leo picked up Edward's plate; Leon, Leselle's.

"We'll help you, Momma," said Leo. "Sit down and rest."

"I'll get you a foot tub of water and put some epsom salt in it so you can soak your feet," said Leon, putting some water on the stove.

"I don't know what'd I do without you boys."

Momma let them take over. She was tired, I could feel it. Since Poppa had been laid off, it was a constant struggle each day. I went hungry many times. Momma was so busy trying to find the peace in the struggle for peace that she'd sometimes forget to take care of herself. Her ankles had blown up, and when Junior made mention of it, she just said that that was what happens when you're expecting a baby.

Poppa was in and out of moods. He'd bring his friends over to the house. Momma would have to wait on them on top of all the other things she had to do. Then later on, Junior would come in from work and Poppa would want to know what was going on down at the mill, "the plant," while adding his two cents' worth along the way.

These were indeed trying times. And Momma was always on guard for anything, expecting that anything to be the worst.

While Momma soaked her feet, Leo and Leon did what little cleaning there was to do. Of course, there was never much. Momma always kept a clean house, but it seemed the farther I got along, the more Momma would clean. Clean the kitchen. Clean the bedrooms. Clean the bathroom. Clean the yard. She kept saying she had to get her house in order before I arrived. That everything had to be just right for it to be just right.

When the water in the foot tub had turned cooler than the breeze, Leon took it away and brought out a washcloth and Momma's house shoes. He dried off her left foot, then the right, handling each as if it were treasure. When they were dry, he slid her house shoes onto her feet. This was a rarity. Momma normally never put on her house shoes during the day. They were for the end of the day when there was nothing else she could think of to do. Even putting on her house shoes became something to do, instead of something comforting. But today, she didn't resist. Her mind seemed elsewhere. The difference between the fantasy and the reality was the moment in which they each occurred.

Momma took Ida Mae's letter and walked out to the porch. She eased her way onto the swing. Leon climbed on one side, Leo the other. She pressed the letter next to me and we all rocked on that swing for a long time, enjoying what in church they call a moment of silence.

Amen.

*   *   *

The day had been pleasant. The twins rarely needed or longed for any unnecessary attention and in being that way, rarely got it, especially not from Poppa. They had been companions since birth, and Momma enjoyed this time with herself and me. She sat on the swing for much of the day sewing me a jumper from the dress she had not worn since Halloween. When she could no longer bear the stillness of the house, she got out the washtub and did some washing. When she took the clothes out to hang on the line, the twins appeared from their game of hide-and-seek.

"Momma? Momma, are we evil?"

"What?" Momma realized that this was something that she would have to listen to. It wasn't an occasion that would be handled by a one-word stock answer, sending them on their merry ways. No. This called for her full attention. "What did you say?"

"Evil? Are we evil?"

"Evil? No, Leo. Now, where in the world would you get a notion like that?"

"After Sunday school one time, we heard somebody say not to mess with us, sayin' 'cuz we were evil. That we had bad blood and that's why we were the way we were and that anyone that we didn't like, we'd put the evil eye on them and that Gram had been a witch and put hexes on people she didn't like and that she passed it on to us before she died. They said we put it on the girl that drowned in the creek last year—that's why she died so young."

Momma stopped putting the sheet on the line for a second and looked at the two, each wide-eyed and waiting for an answer, waiting to hear if the blood running through their bodies made them evil. Momma slowly finished spreading out the sheet, putting a clothespin on each end, placing the extra ones in the clothespin bag that hung in between the clothes drying in a helpful breeze. She raised the stick that held the line so the clothes would be high enough so as the cleanliness she created could remain free of the filth that existed in the soil on her sons' feet. She took them by the hand and we all went underneath the sheet and sat there like it was a teepee, like in the stories Momma would sometimes tell us about the Indians.

"Well, you're at an age now that people start changin'. Sometimes people say things because they hear others sayin' them. Now, just because people say things doesn't mean they know of what they speak," said Momma, looking at the twins and then out at the sheet like it was a window she could see through. "I just want you all to be strong for Momma. Okay? I know it's hard at times, but just try to understand that at times people say mean things for no good reason. Because they want to fit in, they feel that sayin' somethin'—anythin'—is better than havin' nothin' to say. They believe silence is a sign of not knowin'. But you just have to hold your head up high. Your gram always used to say, 'Fittin' in doesn't mean bein' accepted.' Stay above it. The both of you, you hear?"

The boys nodded yes. Though Momma was saying what seemed simple, she was saying it in an adult tone, a way she felt they could understand.

"But they say bad things about you, too—"

"But we tell them to never they mind," said Leo, cutting his brother off and giving him an eye for saying too much.

"Well, don't either of you worry a crumb about what they say about me. Your momma's a big girl and she can handle herself."

"You mean you gonna come down to Sunday school and beat 'em up?"

"No, Leon. Mommas don't fight." Momma stopped for a minute, then started laughing. "Though, I did fight once. But only once."

The twins looked at Momma like she'd said, "Let's go to the moon," and sitting under that sheet, out of view except for what could be seen below, it was like we *had* gone to the moon.

"I wasn't much older than you are now, if you can believe that. This girl at vacation Bible school, Yolanda Payne—Yolanda Payne, that was her name. You see, her last name was spelled with a *y*, but she always spelt it with an *i* when she wrote it out because she liked the attention she got by doing it.

"Well, Yolanda had been saying all kinds of such

and such. She called me a high-yellow . . . well, a name that didn't sit quite right with me. Especially not at vacation Bible school. She said I thought I was 'Miss Somethin' ' because I had 'good hair,' and that ever'body knew how I got it. Yolanda just kept on, and ever'day, she had somethin' smart to say, even though her mouth wouldn't know a smart thought if she swallowed it.

"I tried to pay her no never mind just like I told the two of you to do. I tried to walk away, turn my back to silliness. But one day at snack time, all the kids in the churchyard stopped drinkin' their juice and came over to where we were standin', because *Miss Yolanda Payne* had decided she was going to spread it around that she was goin' to get me at the break.

"So there we were. She called me a few names and then she ended it by sayin'—she said, "And yo' greasy, high-yellow mammy, too . . .' "

Momma got up off the ground and stood under the sheet. The boys followed her lead. It was like she wasn't Momma at all, but that young girl in the churchyard, sermons ago.

". . . and ever'body went crazy when she said that, because when you talked about somebody's momma, that was always throwin' hands words. You could say whatever you mind about somebody's poppa, but not their momma; that meant a right-out battle.

"So when I heard her say that, it really hurt me

because ever'body in the churchyard was laughin' at me and cluckin' like chickens, 'Bahk, bahk, bahk.' Which didn't bother me one iota. Mind you, I wasn't about to let her talk about your gram like that, and I started to swell up. I stood there, then ol' Shifty Moore—that ol' no-account troublemaker, he was so shifty he couldn't make a steady shadow at noontime. But you could rest assured if there was goin' to be a fight, he'd be the first one there to get it up and goin'.

"Well, he came runnin' out of the crowd and got between me and Yolanda and said, 'Bad man, put yo' hand on top.' "

"But you ain't no man, Momma," says Leo.

"Not *ain't*. But, no, I'm not, Leo. You see that's just what people said when two people were about to get into a fight. It showed that you weren't afraid of the other person. So Shifty stuck out his ashy ol' hand and Yolanda slapped her hand down on his first. Then ever'body turned and looked at me, waitin' to see if I was gonna be the bad man that put my hand on top. But I was so swelled up mad, I did this motion as if I was goin' to slap my hand down on Yolanda's, but instead, I swung for her head and grabbed a handful of hair."

Momma grabbed the sheet and the clothespins snapped from each end, finding their way back to earth.

"You see, your Auntie Ida Mae taught me that one. She said where the head goes, the body will follow, and Ida Mae knew—too well—because didn't a day pass by without somebody saying somethin' about Ida Mae and her momma. She told me one time that you either stand there all day waitin' for somebody to pass the first lick, walkin' around in circles, or you can skip all the hymns beforehand and go straight to the collection. Because in a fight, it's always the head and not the body that people go for.

"So I pulled at her hair till she was near 'bout baldheaded and we rolled all over the ground like two boys. Of course, when girls fight, they fight harder than boys, because we rarely get to. So when we do, we make up for all the times we wish we could have but didn't." By this time, the sheet had fallen to the ground, and the twins started rolling around like they were fighting.

"Take that, and that," they screamed, fighting a schoolmate that wasn't there. Momma and me were punching at a shirt on a line, Poppa's favorite. When Momma ran low on wind, I could feel the life in me like never before—as if the beat of my heart carried the weight of us both.

We all sat on the sheet, but Momma didn't miss a beat with telling the story. She could always tell a good story. She says that when you're an only child, telling stories becomes secondhand to you because most of the time you have to tell them to yourself. I was to be Auntie Clariece's only child, so I guessed I'd soon know.

"Finally, Yolanda and I got broken up, but I had that hair like a underwater turtle, and as the sayin' goes, those turtles don't let go till lightnin' strikes! And boys, I'm here to tell you, on that day the sun was shinin' and there wasn't a cloud to be found," said Momma with a hearty laugh. It was the first time in a long while that I'd heard—felt—her laugh like that. From here, sometimes it's hard to tell the difference in the feeling between laughing and crying, but this time I knew it was laughing. I just knew.

"Well, I felt like the queen of England, and ever'-body was huddled around me, sayin' that I won. Nobody was around Yolanda Payne with a *y* except her cousin, cockeyed Jesse. But if he wasn't her kin, I know cockeyed Jesse would have been around me, too. I heard him try and comfort her by sayin' that she got the last lick, but I knew that wasn't so, and so did she."

"Was you happy you beat her up, Momma?"

"Were, Leo."

"Were you happy you beat her up?"

"Well, I must admit I was feelin' mighty fine. Ever'body was treatin' me with respect that day. But you see, I had no clue as to what was comin'. You see, after school, I walked home just all full of myself, head big as a pumpkin. But that quickly turned into a jack-o'-lantern. When I got home, there was your gram sittin' on the porch, waitin'. Of course, she had already heard all about it. News tends to travel faster than a lightnin' bolt when your child does somethin' wrong and other mommas want to bring it to your attention.

"But there was your gram, just sittin' there readin' a book all pretty and proper, being her usual ladylike self. She didn't say one word. She politely closed her book, got up, and walked in the house. She had an expression on her face that told me I was to follow. She walked to the chiffarobe, where she kept the few things of your grandfather's since the—the funeral—and pulled out a belt. It was thick—well not so much thick, but wide—and my eyes got big. Your gram had never raised a hand to me. She'd always threaten to, but she never would. No. Your gram preferred to pinch or put me on restriction, which meant sendin' me to my room.

"Well, I tried to open my mouth to tell her that I was defendin' her good name, but no good words would come out because all I could think about was that belt. Gram said that she'd have to use the belt instead of a switch because of my thin skin, bein' that she didn't want to make any 'showin' marks' due to the fact she didn't want people knowin' her business.

"She said all this like she was sayin' it to your papa's suit jackets, never turnin' around to look at me. See, that's how your gram would do. Whenever she turned her back to you, you knew you were in for it. I still couldn't say anythin'. She said she'd heard what happened that day at vacation Bible school and that she wanted me to know that she was very disappointed in me. 'Very disappointed.' When your gram said that, it hurt me real bad. I didn't ever want to disappoint her. But to hear her say it hurt. She told me she knew it was hard on me, but just because I was a bit different didn't give me—or anyone else, for that matter—just cause to go around takin' swings at folks; I was a young lady and should carry myself as such and know that the only swingin' to be done was to be done by her.

"And she meant it, too. Because havin' said that, she started walkin' toward me with the belt and, against my better judgment, I started runnin'. I ran around the house, around the yard, ever'where. And my momma—your gram—took off after me faster than a squirrel during squirrel season.

"With one hand, she hiked up her dress and with the other, she had the belt. Even in midstride, she never missed her target. A bull's-eye ever' shot. I didn't think it was possible for a grown woman— let alone your gram—to run that fast, but she did, and she tore me up. I think that my makin' her run after me made her give me a few extra licks, just for her efforts.

"When she was done, she didn't even have to tell me to go to my room, because I marched in there anyway. I didn't want to have to look at her. I was in my room just a-mouthin' off, thinkin' she couldn't hear me. But of course she could, and she told me to hush up or she'd come in there and wear out my 'li'l narrow behind' again. Thinkin' back on it now, it sounded like she was laughin' when she said it. Then, I thought she was cryin'. Sometimes it's kind of hard to tell the difference."

Momma paused for a second, then chuckled, looking at each of the boys, as if seeing them for the first time after a long absence, running her hands along their hair, the hair Yolanda—and probably kids in their Sunday school class—would call good hair.

"Goodness gracious. Look at this sheet," said Momma, getting off the white sheet that was now covered with dirt and grass stains from their make-believe battle.

"It's all dirty," said Leo, looking at his footprints on the sheet.

Momma balled up the sheet and the three of them and me started toward the house.

"Is it ruint, Momma?"

"No, baby. It's not ruined. God made grass. God made dirt. Dirt and grass can't hurt. Momma'll wash it away. Don't worry about that. Momma'll take care of ever'thin'."

The day had been so wonderful that Momma had forgotten about Poppa, forgotten about Teacake's cow, and forgotten about Clariece's visit tomorrow. But a forget-me-not soon reminded her. She could hear Poppa coming up the walk, he and Teacake singing, stumbling over the whitewashed stones that lined the walk to the house. She went to the screen door. Edward and Leselle were walking silently in front of them with Junior, the same as before, trailing behind.

Poppa climbs up on the steps and sits in his rocker; Teacake, on the swing. Junior walks through the screen door and doesn't say anything.

"Teacake, since you don't have a hat, why don't you rest yo' leg for a spell? Stay a while," says Poppa, laughing up a storm on what had otherwise been a sunny, beautiful day.

"Yeah, I'll rest it, awright. Right up yo' ass."

"Watch yo' tongue now. I'll tell Anna to go in there and get my jar of termites and set 'em loose out here on ya."

Poppa is talking loud and Teacake is matching him, just like the women feeling the Spirit at a Sunday service. Edward and Leselle stay real still on the steps, like that's what they're supposed to do. Edward is shaking, though, and Leselle has his arm around his big brother's shoulders. They aren't fighting, not now.

"Edward, Leselle, go on in the house and take a bath; get ready for supper," says Momma.

"Dem's my boys there. My boys! Teacake, look at 'em. Spendin' the whole day wit they Poppa. Likes li'l men. That's how it's s'posed to be," says Poppa, trying to get up and go toward them, but, unable to gain his balance, he falls back into his rocker. Edward rushes past Poppa without looking at him and goes into the house. Leselle follows. Poppa laughs like it's a game.

"Go on, now. Go on and get ready for supper and tell Leon and Leo to do the same," says Momma, just loud enough for them to hear.

"J. T., it's time for supper. Teacake, join us for supper?"

"Nah! Hell nah! He ain't joinin' us for nothin'. Nigga'll eat us out of house and home. Anyway, we ain't near 'bout finished wit our day just yet. We gonna go down to the Nail and have us some fun."

"Nigga, you been havin' fun outta my pocket all day long," says Teacake, spit gathering in his mouth as it always seems to do. Poppa once said that it did that because Teacake was full of hot air. "Ya damn right, we goin' to the Nail—and you buyin', you no-good, triflin' somethin' 'nother. 'Cuz if we don't, this here leg of mine will be yo' problem."

And just as they came, they get up and go down the path arm in arm, toward the Rusty Nail, one staggering because he has to, the other out of need. Momma watched them disappear into the darkness, and I couldn't feel laughter or tears; I couldn't feel anything from here.

Momma went in and finished the cooking. The twins set the table. We all sat down and had grace. Junior seemed out of sorts and inside himself. Momma tried to coax out what was eating him.

"Junior, did the cow pass the calf today?" said

Momma, passing him the cabbage greens and salt meat.

"We got to his place, come to find out, Teacake don't even have no cow. He don't even have no chickens. Nothin' but that shotgun house full of nothin'. When we got over there, he and some of the other men that got laid off from the mill was there hangin' out. They sat 'round eggin' me on all day and drankin' corn liquor like it was ice tea." Junior looked up from his food. " 'Scuse me; I ain't hungry."

Junior pushed away from the table and went out to the porch. Momma looked at Edward and Leselle, but they didn't say anything. The two were very different when Poppa wasn't around. It was like they didn't have to impress anybody; they could just be. They were respectful to Momma for the most part, but there was no doubting that they were Poppa's favorites. They were the only ones that resembled him. The twins looked nothing like him; they were definitely from Momma's side of the family. Their hazel eyes, sharp features, and small "white folks" lips reminded Poppa of that every day. We found out from Cousin Lucille—she wasn't a real cousin; it was just that she had known Poppa since he was a li'l boy and so everybody called her cousin. She had a lazy eye, so you never knew which way she was looking. So sometimes she'd ask somebody a question and nobody would answer because nobody was sure who she was talking to.

When she paid a visit once, she said that though
Edward and Leselle looked like Poppa, Junior was
the male image of Poppa's momma.

It was at the kitchen table, when everybody was
sitting there, that all the mixtures presented
themselves.

... Today, I pulled out an old postcard from
you—the first one you sent me. I didn't pull it out
because I'd forgotten what it said, but because it
seemed like so long ago since you sent it. I know
the days up there probably just run together, but
here, every day counts.

"Wish you was here."

When I got it, the first thing I thought was *Wish
you were here.* Were, *Ida Mae.*

I'm still always trying to make things right. I
didn't even look at the picture on the front until
much later. Usually, with a postcard, it's more
about the picture than the words on the back.
But when I did take a moment to look at it, Bessie
Smith was smiling. It gave me hope . . .

Like Junior, Auntie Clariece was also the walking
image of Poppa's momma, as she kept telling us
when she was here last Christmas. She never let an
opportunity go by without reminding everybody
that people used to tell her it looked like her
momma had "spit her out."

That Christmastime, the first one of my existence,

was the first time I ever caught a feel of the woman
that Poppa wanted to raise me. He still didn't know
about me then, but time would soon put the pieces
together, and Auntie was to play a major part in
this puzzle.

Momma said Poppa always loved Christmastime,
and life was always good when that time of year
inched its way around on the calendar, a gift from
Tucker's Market that hung on the kitchen wall.

It was the night after Poppa had brought the tree
in from out of the woods near the lumber mill.
Poppa always likes to go out and choose the tree
and surprise everybody. He'd drag it back, where
everybody would be waiting to string it with popcorn and cranberries and whatever else the boys
had come up with. That night, he had found an
especially pleasing tree and was in a good mood,
playful even. He would hug Momma, pressing
close, for I had yet to widen the space between
them. The boys would come up and circle us. Everything seemed so right and I was pleased that this
man was going to be my poppa. Momma even said
to me, "That's your Poppa there. You're just what
he's been waitin' for. I know it. You can bring the
spirit back into him. I know you can."

Poppa was sitting in the living room and all the
boys were around his chair. They were laughing
and carrying on. It seemed like the most normal
thing in the world to me, for it was all I knew up
to that point.

Christmas was falling on a Sunday that year, which meant a lot of work for Momma. She and I were in the kitchen, cooking away. She would cook and nibble, hands going every whicha way, timing it all till everything came out picture perfect. There was pecan pie and peach cobbler and sweet-potato pie and poundcake and, and, and, and. Ever' so often, she'd sneak a look out in the living room and there'd be Poppa on the floor wrestling with the boys. Even Leo and Leon joined in, and their laughter could be heard even in the dried, rustling cornstalks in the field behind the house.

Poppa would lay flat on his stomach, letting them all pile on his back, then he'd slowly rise till he was up on all fours, each of them sliding off as he rose toward his peak. Of course the boys would make a big racket, but it was a noise that didn't sit in your head. You wanted it louder, because the noise mixed up a recipe for joy.

At the height of the boys' screaming fit, Poppa would grab two of them, one in each hand, picking them up from the back of their britches until they dangled in the air like chinaberries hanging from a branch in spring. He asked them if they'd been good boys and they'd say, in between their laughter and screams, that they had and then yell for Poppa to put them down so he wouldn't drop them. But deep down, down where it counts, they didn't want him to put them down. They wanted him to hold them for as long as he would. A good time was being had.

While two of the boys were dangling from those hands, the others would attack one of his legs or jump on his back. Even Junior, big as he was, played along, and Poppa would walk through the living room, dragging his sons, all of them, along with him.

Christmastime was when he became a child again, and it pleased everybody, especially Momma. It was times like these times that gave her hope for me.

The screams that slid throughout the house that Christmastime were easy on the ear and the laughter served as kindling. Then a knock came at the door, and the wind quickly changed its direction, blowing out the flame. Christmas always comes in winter, but never is its chill like that which now came in the form of Auntie Clariece.

"Clariece," said Poppa. The laughter that had been shaping his face vanished, to be replaced by something time had not allowed me to make out or understand.

"Well, you goin' to stand there with all those boys all up on you like you nursin' 'em, or are you goin' to invite your only sister in?"

Her voice was something else. Highbrow. It was like she was over talking to sound different from everybody else. "Making airs" is what I believe I've heard it called. The sounds came from out of her mouth, but the words slid down her nose as she watched each one till they fell upon those at which they were aimed. Whether the words she used were the right ones or not never seemed to matter to her. It was the delivery and the sound of them that she cherished. Momma never corrected her, aware some things aren't worth changing.

"Sorry, Clariece." Poppa pushed open the screen door and Clariece—Auntie Clariece, the woman that I now know is to be my mother—seemed to be on overtime and didn't miss a step or a beat. She had arrived—and her presence was felt.

"Li'l Man, get that silly look off that face of yourn and bring my bag in. I know you weren't *suspectin'* me. But I happened to be in your neck of the woods and, bein' the holiday season and all, I knew you wouldn't mind if I paid you and yours a visit for the evening. That is fine, Li'l Man, itn't it?"

"Sho, Clariece. Whatever you likes," mumbled Poppa, shaking the boys off of him and picking up Auntie's bag.

"See, James is preachin' a revival and he stayed on down there in Eudora. Even though it's the biggest city in Welty County, it's nothin' 'pared to up north. 'Sides, I was tired of bein' the preacher's wife, so I said, 'James, give me some money, 'cause I'm not stayin' in this li'l hillbilly, stinkin' town one more minute,' and I came on here to be with my brother. I drove myself. Did you see our car? I can drive now, you know. Bet you didn't know that. Not many colored folks in these here parts got a nice car like that, if any at all. You can look at it later if you please, but be sure not to touch it. We just had it polished, and prints from greasy hands stand out like a person stealin' from the collection plate. I hope none of these countrified folk 'round here take a notion to get 'round it. Then again, the good Lawd knows you ain't got no neighbors in shoutin' distance of this place, so that ain't very likely, now is it? Pity. It might do them some good to see how *exceptable* people live. I suppose y'all still walkin' ever'where. Figures. Class can't be bought."

Gram had offered to buy Momma—and Poppa—a car long ago, but Poppa wouldn't have it. Said "we" didn't need it, that if things weren't in walking distance, then it was no use to "us."

Auntie took a breath only to look around and comb the house, then burning whatever came out, she started up again.

"Where's that wife of yourn? I been here a good minute awready and haven't been offered a thing. Somebody 'round here needs to learn some . . . Lawd, look at these here chilren! Just as skinny as they wanna be. She pro'bly think she's too good to cook a meal. I told you from the get-go about that gal. I'm just thankful Ma Dear—Lawd rest her soul—ain't here to make witness of how you turned out.

"Junior?! Junior, my word. Boy, look at you. The last time I saw you, you was knee-high to a grasshopper. Now you nearly a grown man. At least they'll be one real man 'round here. Wouldn't you say? I know you drivin' the womens crazy. But watch yourself out there, boy. Don't *except* anything that walk by. Those young gals out there nowaday ain't no good. They all just as fast as they wanna be. They'll soak you up like dry ground waitin' for rain. And I'm here to tell you it don't take but a moment to plant the seed. Half of 'em would probably lie to St. Peter if they thought it would get 'em into heaven. Boy, what's wrong with you? Can't you see I'm sittin' here talkin' to you? You ain't sayin' a word. Where's your manners, boy?

"Li'l Man, what's wrong with this here boy? Cat got his tongue? I guess now that he all big, he smellin' his groins now. That's how they get, you know? Nowaday, they think they's too old to mind they elders. Boy, let your Auntie Clariece tell you you ain't never too big for a good ol' country bootie whuppin'. Never. 'Course, ain't nobody 'round here to make you mind. But I'm here now. Your gran'-momma raised your Poppa by herself, and when she died, I took over the burden. And let me tell you, your daddy knew his place. Ain't that right, Li'l Man?"

"Yessum. I means, that's right, Clariece." Poppa sat down like he had been bad and was sent there until told otherwise.

"Boys, take a break; you gonna wear your poppa out," said Momma, coming into the living room. She thought the racket was from the boys playing.

Momma's tone, too, changed when she saw Auntie Clariece. "Oh, Clariece. I didn't know you were comin'. I mean, Joe didn't tell . . . I was in the kitchen tryin' to get a head start on the bakin' for Christmas and the boys was out here playin'. I heard some talkin', but I just thought it was them carryin' on. You know how boys can get. Can I get you somethin'? Junior, get your Auntie somethin' warm to drink, take away the chill in the air."

Auntie Clariece walked over to Momma and peeked in the kitchen. Momma had flour on her face and apron. Auntie Clariece told her it was hard to tell if that was flour or if she just wasn't feeling well, being that she "rarely had any color" in her anyway.

At supper that evening, things stayed pretty much the same. Auntie Clariece carried the conversation. When the food was on the table, everybody came in the kitchen. But before Poppa could get to what everybody knew as his place at the table, Auntie Clariece took roost and no one, not even Poppa, dared move her from her nest.

"Hasn't your momma taught you two not to stare at peoples?" Leon and Leo looked at one another, and then Leo said that they weren't staring. Auntie Clariece stopped in midchew and spit out the food she had in her mouth into her napkin. "Don't you talk back to me. I refuse to sit here in my own brother's house and be sassed by some li'l half-breed—"

"Clariece, the boys don't mean no harm. They just haven't seen you in some time and they—"

"Uh, uh, uh," said Auntie Clariece, cutting Momma off. "I know you ain't about to sit there and make excuses. Now I see why they is the way they is. You obviously don't discipline them. In my day, a child sass back to a grown folk, they had better be ready for what followed. They'd get a hidin' right then and there, and another one when they got home. That's not to mention the backhand slap they'd get across their mouth as the words were coming out.

"And I tell you another thing: if me and the Reverend James Caldwell was to have chilren, they wouldn't be *omitted* to stare at people like they was crazy. That, you could be sure of. It's downright disrespectful. Look at 'em. Just sittin' there eyein' me like . . . like I don't know what! Li'l Man, I've lost my appetite. Where am I gonna be sleepin'? I'm weak from my drive. And you know I can't sleep on no couch. My back won't have it."

Auntie got up from the table, taking a toothpick with her. She used that toothpick like it was a magic stick and waved it around with every sentence. And when the spell was cast, Poppa said not to worry, that she could sleep in his and Momma's room.

"Well, I guess that'll be *proficient*. You ain't still wettin' the bed, now is you? I tell you, Li'l Man used to wet the bed so much, Ma Dear would have to beat him to get him to stop, and he still would do it. You wanna hear somethin' funny?—I bet you forgot about this, Li'l Man—but one mornin', Ma Dear tied him up to a tree in the front yard in nothin' but his drawers, so ever'body that passed could see he had soiled hisself. I tell you, I can't even count the number of sheets and spreads that boy ruint. He'd try and hide it. Try buryin' his underwear in the wastebasket, but you just can't bury that stench. You ain't still doin' that, is you?''

"No'm. I means, no, Clariece. The sheets clean.''

The first night I met the woman meant to be my mother, we slept on a pallet Momma made on the floor, but I know Momma didn't really sleep. She watched Poppa tossing and turning on the couch that wasn't big enough for him anymore.

Momma said she had planned on telling Poppa about me that night. But Auntie Clariece's visit stole the words away from her.

After supper, the boys helped Momma clear the dishes and she ushered them off to bed. Poppa was still at the Nail with Teacake, and Junior was still outside on the porch. His plate stayed untouched. Momma left it wrapped up and put it on the stove for him to come back to later. After she washed up, she went in to wish the younger boys a good night's rest. She squatted—I was growing so she could no longer bend—and kissed each of them, from the youngest up. Leo (he had been born thirteen min-

utes after Leon), Leon, Leselle, then Edward. But
Edward held on longer than usual. When he did let
go, Momma held on for a few heartbeats more. In
the same motion that she let go, she blew out the
candle on the night stand near their bed. There was
that instant of darkness where everything was pitch
black, but soon Momma's eyes adjusted and she
could see the four figures of her children, safe in
bed. It was this time each night that made getting
through the day worthwhile.

She opened the bedroom door and a stream of
light from the living room entered, then shortened
to nothing as she edged the door shut behind her.
She pressed her body against the door. We stood
there for a minute, and for the first time that day,
she placed her hand on me. And it felt good, to
both of us.

... I worry about Junior. He's grown up so.
He's no little boy anymore. My first-born is a
man, too old to know he's too young to regret.
The young should never regret when there's so
much life left for them to live. Do you have any
regrets? I don't. Not yet ...

Momma walks to the porch where Junior is sitting on the steps. Gnats busy themselves around the
porch light, but Momma, paying no attention to
their scurrying, walks to the swing and sits.

"Nice evening," says Momma. "Don't you think?"

"S'pose." Junior looks out into the distance. Momma sits between breaths, waiting for him to say what it is he needs to get off his ever-forming chest. She doesn't have to wait long.

"I'm tired, Momma."

"It's been a long day. You should—"

"I don't mean that way. I mean I'm tired of thangs bein' like they are. He don't give two cents 'bout nothin' and nobody. You should've seen him, Momma. Today at Teacake's. He was sittin' 'round with all those bums, and to show out for them, he offered me a drink. I told him I didn't want none, and he started sayin' that's 'cuz I wasn't no man and that I shouldn't forget that he still was the 'king of the castle.' Even if I had the job down at the plant or not, he was still the king, and I best to not forget it.

"After a while, I got sick of hearin' it, so I went off, just walkin' 'round to get away from it. I wasn't even gone for long—an hour's time at most. I should have just stayed there . . ." Junior's voice trails to nothing. He looks as if he's scanning his mind to make sure he believes what he'd seen, for it seems beyond belief to him. But as the day replays before him, his disgust finds the words, as if it's all happening for the first time, in this instant.

"When I got back, Edward was throwin' up and all them men was just sittin' there watchin' him,

doin' nothin' 'bout him. Just hootin' and hollerin'
like they was chilren. Poppa had made him drink
that corn liquor. I couldn't believe it . . .''

Junior stands from the step and throws the stone
he's been playing with into the beyond. Where it
ended up was not to be seen, but the faint sound
of its landing assured him that it reached someplace
safe. Someplace away from where he stood. Junior
turns to Momma. We're still on the swing, listening,
as Junior needs to say these things more for himself
than for us.

"Poppa kept sayin', 'You a man now, Edward;
you a man now.' Just screamin' it, Momma. 'You a
man now.' All his buddies was hootin' and hollerin', hootin' and hollerin'. Leselle started cryin',
so Poppa screamed at him to hush up and that he
didn't want him cryin' like no li'l punk in front of
ever'body. Poppa just sat there, laughin' at him. I
gotta do somethin', Momma. I just . . . I . . . I'm
goin' crazy, and I—I'm just sick of him and . . . and
his . . . his goddamn—"

Before the word was completely out of Junior's
mouth, Momma stands up with a swiftness not recently seen, like I'm not even there. She moves so
fast that the swing doesn't sway underneath.

"Come here," says Momma. "I said come here."

Junior and Momma move toward each other.
Momma grabs him by the collar.

"In the seventeen years of your life, have you

ever—ever—heard me use a foul word in front of you? In front of any of you? Have you?"

Junior doesn't speak, can't. Momma hadn't shouted, but the pain roars from way down where I lay. She has a look that wears on longer than a slap. Junior probably would rather have a slap, for a slap hurts for a moment, but that look on Momma's face will sting his heart for a lifetime. Tears swell in the corner of Momma's eyes like water from a rainstorm fighting to get over the levee, stopping just before the break, saving what little damage is left to be done by the winds of the storm.

"At least give me that same respect. Do you hear me, Junior? Do you? I don't mean to have to repeat myself on that again. I've never asked you for anythin', but will you give me that?"

"Yes, ma'am," says Junior, just below a whisper, his Adam's apple bobbing, leaving him with a stutter.

Momma lets go of him and it appears as if Junior's feet touch the porch again. She runs her hands along his shirt, smoothing the wrinkles her grip made. That done, she walks back to the swing. And with the same sense of stillness, she sits. Junior stands like he's been stung by something, something that flows through his being until he was completely paralyzed. Now, the post near the steps supported not only the porch. Then, as if the previous moment had not occurred, Momma tells Junior that she's sorry and she understands, but she won't stand for his bad-mouthing Poppa. She says that she knows times are rough and that they—we—will get through them together. As a family.

Momma gives Junior a smile and motions for him to come to her. He walks to the swing and sits by her side, slowly regaining control of his muscles. Momma puts her left hand into his right and we all sway back and forth till the words fall into place.

"I know Poppa wants you to give the baby to Auntie Clariece and Uncle James." Momma's lips don't part, but her grip on Junior's hand strengthens. "I just don't understand, Momma. How can you let him do it? All the thangs he puts you through, but you still put up with it. It ain't right."

"Well, Junior, you're gettin' to the age that you'll be takin' on a wife, or courtin' someone, and you'll feel somethin' that you've never felt before. Your Poppa is a good man. But even good men have their own problems to deal with. There's a sayin': 'Even the weakest of dogs are too proud to let you see them lick their wounds.' Remember that, because you're bound to have your share. Sometimes you hurt the ones you love because of things that have nothin' to do with them. If and when you truly love someone, that's somethin' you have to know.

"Some things can't be understood by all because all the information isn't there to help you find your way. What you're sayin' when you love someone is you're willin' to take on ever'thin' that comes with them. Of course, there's no way to know it all. It takes time.

"It's kind of like when you hear someone singin' a song in church. And you can sing the song along with them, word for word, and feel mighty fine, and you start to smile. But when you're by yourself, you realize somethin's missing. And as much as it frustrates you, you need help, because the words don't fall into place. You only know parts and pieces. Until those parts and pieces come together, you don't really know the whole thing. The tune has to be enough."

"Do you still love him?" says Junior, looking at Momma. She doesn't face him. She just keeps looking straight ahead, almost as if the gnats have asked the question and are waiting for a reply. I feel a big breath given to me and, though she doesn't say it, at the peak of that breath rests a . . .

. . . We all have so much to learn, but when do we get to pass it on? When do we stop protecting and begin informing?

I learned something from you every moment that we spent together, but it took me years to realize it. Did you learn anything from me?

Can people take and take and take without realizing it's not necessarily being taken, but given? I pray you're learning something new. I'm trying . . .

"Come on now, Ida Mae. You can do it," said Anna when she would pass on her teachings to Ida Mae. *"Go on now. You live in . . . ?*

"Girl, dat's easy. I live in Miss'ip'i."

"No, Ida Mae. Spell it out like I told you. Come on, just sing it out. Remember?"

"Nah."

"M, I, crooked letter, crooked letter, i . . ."

"Crooked letter, crooked letter, i . . ."

Ida Mae joined in to finish it, "Humpback, Humpback, i."

"See, you knew it. You just needed someone to help you along," said Anna. As she and Ida Mae skipped along the creek, singing together, they yelled about the crooked letters and the humpbacks that spelled home.

5

We're up. Momma's caressing her coffee cup, but not a drop makes it to her mouth. She's worried this morning, and we didn't get much rest last night. Whenever Momma worries, she cleans. Sometimes it's hard for her to find things to clean because she's already done all that can possibly be done. Maybe it isn't even about cleaning. Maybe it's just about thinking about something else, if just for a spell.

"Your Poppa had a bad dream last night" is what she told me when we got up this morning. When Poppa came back from being with Teacake at the Rusty Nail, he was feeling the spirit, but not that of God, and was being right friendly to Momma while she helped him from the porch to the bedroom.

"I loves you, Anna," Poppa kept slurring just before his head hit the pillow and he fell asleep. "I don't know what I'd do witoutchu."

Momma knew it was the drinks talking. But deep down inside her, deep down where I lay, she prayed there was some truth in it. She knew there was. She knew.

Momma pulled the covers over him to keep the cold of liquor off his skin, numbed of feeling. Of course, Momma had been up waiting for him to get home, just in case he needed something. I was sleeping, but I woke up in the night because I could feel a change in Momma. Poppa was moaning, almost whimpering like a young bird that has fallen from the nest and can only whimper because his wings aren't yet strong enough to lift himself back to the place considered safe.

Poppa was having some bad dream and he kept trying to fend off whatever—whomever—had entered his sleep. His body was tossing and turning and bumping into us. He was telling them "no" and that it wasn't right. He started to kick and roll over, getting all tangled up in the covers. His underclothes were drenched and Momma ran her hand along his back trying to comfort him, like she does me when I kick at her. She knows I don't mean to hurt her. She knows it.

"J. T., J. T.! Wake up, baby," said Momma, shaking him from his restless sleep. As Momma said this, Poppa popped up from his pillow like he had been under water and would have drowned had he been there a second more. He needed air, and he came up gasping. "J. T., you all right?"

Poppa sat there grabbing for a breath as if it were his first. Looking around, almost to assure himself of his whereabouts, he started crying.

Poppa started crying.

"It was her. She was here. In my house," Poppa said. He was talking like he was a child. It was the drunk still seeping out of him. It must have been.

"This is my house. Why she wanna come here and bother me now?"

"Who? Joe, who's botherin' you?" Momma said, holding him in her arms.

"Ma Dear. She came in here, pulled me outta bed, and pushed me in the livin' room. She had a strop with her. And I looked over at you, but you didn't wake up. Anna, it was like you wahn't part of it, like you wahn't there. I knew it was a dream, but I couldn't wake up. She started yellin' at me like I was a child. But in the dream I wahn't. I was grown. But she was still yellin' and hittin' me with the strop. She was mad about somethin', but I didn't know what it was. I don't think it was even nothin' I done. She was just mad. I tried to talk to her, to calm her down, but I knew how she was when she got like this, and the more I tried to say somethin', the madder she got and just kept hittin' me."

Poppa was silent for a second, then he started crying harder, like a baby looking for a nipple in the night. Each word was getting sucked through every breath. Each of those breaths held a silent moment, moments of confusion waiting for that release that would free the sound silenced by yon years. Poppa was hurting inside, and those moments of silence only reminded him of that.

"And I could see my daddy out of the corner of my eye. And he had on the same clothes he had the last day I saw him. The day of the funeral. And I looked like his twin. He was standin' there in the livin' room up against that wall. But he couldn't do nothin'. He just stood there. I yelled for him to help me, and when I yelled out 'Poppa,' Ma Dear grabbed me and put my head 'tween her legs so I wouldn't move and she beat me. She just kept at me with that strop.

"I kept sayin' to myself this weren't happenin', 'cuz I was grown. I was grown now and this was my house. But she kept yellin' at me and hittin' me with that strop. And then she let me go and I fell to the floor. I just sat there, her standin' ovah me.

"She looked 'round the house and said I was no good and I'd 'mounted to nothin', just like she said I would. Just like my 'no-good daddy.' And she got madder. Then she yelled for me to take off my clothes so she could beat me right. I looked for my daddy, and there he was again. He was standin' there, watchin' and cryin'. All Ma Dear had to do was look at him and he knew not to move. She kept screamin' for me to take off my clothes and pullin' at my undershirt till it tore and hittin' me with the strop as she did it. I took off my underpants and was standing there naked. She started hittin' me again and I jus' stood there. Clariece was standing next to her, like a cat, grinnin'.

"Anna—and Anna, about the third time I felt the strop on my back, it didn't hurt me no more. I didn't feel nothin'. No pain, nothin'. It didn't hurt. And I knew I wasn't a li'l boy no more and that this was my house. It didn't hurt no more.

"Then I looked over at my daddy still standin' there, and it hurt me to see it. Before I could tell him how much I missed him and it was awright, my heart swole up and started racin' like it some-time do in a dream. That's when I woke up. I didn't get to tell him it was awright. I didn't get to tell him."

Poppa looked at Momma. The liquored tears that had already fallen left trails down Poppa's face, clearing the way for the ones that followed. His eyes were like those of a li'l boy's pleading for help from a sickness he can't name.

"Anna. Anna, I didn't get to tell him."

Poppa kept saying that over and over, telling Momma he was sorry. The tears seemed to go on and on like a needed rain with no end in sight. Junior knocked on the door. "Momma, ever'thin' awright?"

"Ever'thin's fine, Junior," Momma said through the door, trying to sound comforting. "Ever'thin' is just fine. Now go on back to bed." Poppa still kept saying he was sorry. He curled up next to Momma and me, and Momma held us both till we fell asleep.

". . . Yes," Momma remembered saying after Junior left her side on the swing and went inside. The words echoed inside her like the sound of drums from distant lands. "I don't know how to explain it. But yes, I still love him." And I felt the beat, too.

. . . I've always been told you can tell how a man will treat a woman based on how he treats his mother. But how a mother treats her son can tell you just as much. I see that now. J. T. had two mommas: the one that bore him, then Clariece, the one who took over the job. Now she's waiting to take over again . . .

Poppa is still in bed. I suppose between the liquor and the dream, he's strung out. I can tell Momma is tired. I'd seen Poppa have fits of rage, but I'd never seen him cry. Besides Auntie Clariece mentioning she was the "spitting image" of their momma, that was the first time I'd ever heard Poppa mention his Ma Dear.

"Don't you go worryin' your li'l self about last night, Lisa," Momma says to me as I start to move around. "Your Poppa wasn't himself last night. Or maybe he was. One day maybe you'll understand, but it's a grown-up thing. No need in you worryin' your pretty li'l soul about it, at least not now. Good mornin', Junior. I didn't hear you come in. I was talkin' to li'l . . . just talkin' to myself. Goin' crazy, I guess. How'd you rest?"

"Fine," Junior says, grabbing a coffee cup and looking at Momma like he's looking for a sign of something. "He ain't up?"

"No. I don't reckon he'll be up for a while yet."

"Figures."

"Meanin'?"

"Just that he came in so drunk, I'm suprised he even made it to the door. You pro'bly had to carry him."

"Junior, please, baby. Not today. I can't play the go-between today. Please. And what if he hears you?"

"What if he does? He's pro'bly still full of liquor. I heard you in there cryin' last night. It ain't right the way he treats you. It just ain't right."

"Junior, honey, I told you things aren't always what they seem. He doesn't mean any harm. Honest, he doesn't. You just don't understand."

"From where I'm standin', some things ain't meant for understandin'. And I don't believe, as long as I live, I'll ever understand him," says Junior, walking out the screen door, letting it slam behind in the same way Poppa had done so many times before.

"What's wrong wit him?"

"J. T.! I didn't know you were up."

"Well, there's a lot you don't know."

"I know, J. T., I know," says Momma, pouring the hot coffee. Poppa sits there like nothing had happened, like the drunk had taken last night from him and the pain this morning is in his head, not his heart.

Momma knows not to bring up the subject. She knows how Poppa can be and, for the most part, why. I once heard Momma tell Junior, after a beating from Poppa, that we all had to understand that things get passed on in a family that sometimes aren't meant to be. Things that, though they aren't talked about, are still never forgotten. As long as there is breath in bodies, there will always be reminders.

Today, one of those reminders is due. For the second time, the woman that has arranged to be my momma is to pay a visit. At the same time, Momma has to deal with everything that truly keeps our family together.

6

. . . I know you don't much care for the notion of church. That's the one thing you and Joseph have in common. But before I go to bed and the first thing I do when I wake up is thank God. It's the Christian thing to do. Right after I thank God, I thank my momma. My momma's gone, but I still pray to God. They've become one and the same.

Will li'l Lisa ever be able to thank her momma—either of them? . . .

Auntie Clariece and Uncle James weren't due until late in the afternoon. The house seemed heavy; the cinder blocks that held it up would have crumbled had anymore pressure presented itself. It was as if everyone knew what this visit was about. The boys busied themselves keeping out of Momma's hair. Though a drop had not fallen, the house smelled of rain. A storm was coming.

Momma took a washtub out to the back porch and placed it at the corner so it could catch some rainwater. As if it had waited for her command, down it came. Not at all drop after drop, but seemingly all at once, causing a sheet of rain that confined us to the back porch.

The back porch was our place and rarely did anyone come back there. Momma would often talk about how she and Ida Mae had sat out there for hours on end. And even if Poppa came through the front, the slam of the screen door served as the warning sign, giving Ida Mae ample time to run out to the cornfield and hide till Momma could get Poppa's attention, leaving Ida Mae to make her quick getaway. Yes, the back porch was our place, and today it only meant that much more.

The rain tap-danced on the roof of tin, making soothing sounds. When each drop had tapped out, down it slid, diving into the washtub. From the porch, we could watch the sun-scorched Johnson grass sipping the moisture and slowly turning, yet again, to its deep green, quenching its thirst for life. The cornstalks stood at attention and everything, through the grayness of the rain, seemed clear.

The porch was where Momma came to talk to me out loud without anyone thinking she was crazy. Sometimes she'd say *she* thought she was crazy.

Poppa had gone off to Teacake's, and Junior had gone out somewhere. "I just need to get away for a while," Junior had said.

Momma hoped the rain was treating them as well as it was us.

"I wish you could have met your gram. She was the best. It took me so long to know it, but she was a good, strong woman, even when it wasn't right to be. But will it ever be right to be? Sometimes we're not given a choice in the matter. I hope by your time, if the Lord's willin', things will be better. She was beautiful, too. You don't really think that kind of thing about your own. You just see a long line of the same thing with a speck of difference sprinkled here and there.

"I miss her. I wish I could've had a sister. I guess Ida Mae was the closest thing I had to one. Your gram acted like she didn't like her, but I knew somewhere in her heart she did. They were just too much alike is all—alike, differently: both strong. No matter where I was, one of them was always there, watchin'. That's probably why your gram made such a fuss about my spendin' time with Ida Mae, but never really forbid me to do it. She knew Ida Mae might do what and what not, but she also knew she'd watch out for me, takin' the harm upon herself when it came my way.

"But your poppa, he claimed he never liked Ida Mae. She scared him as much as Gram did, but for different reasons. He had to respect Gram because she was an elder, and my momma, and for other things not worth mentionin'. But with Ida Mae, it was somethin' more. He knew if I knew it, then Ida Mae knew it. And you see, men are proud bein's. They don't like anybody knowin' that they need help. Help is a form of weakness, and the more people know you're weak, the less they think of you. At least that seems to be the way they think.

"You feel that mist, li'l Lisa? It feels nice, doesn't it? Mist is good for you. It moistens the skin when it's dry. It's God's way of takin' care of not just plants, but us, too. Your gram always used to talk like that. She wasn't a God-fearin' woman, but she didn't mind givin' Him credit for things that brought her joy. She had faith in the good of things. She had a way of seein' things like nobody else. I remember her sayin' one day, 'Ever'body wants to go to heaven, but nobody wants to die.'

"She'd be proud of you. If she said she was goin' to do somethin', you could rest assured she would. She'd say, 'If the Lord is willin' and the creek don't rise . . .' Oh, li'l Lisa, I miss her. There's nothin' like a mother's love, and when you don't have it, you realize it more.

"Your grandfather was killed when I was young. White men thought he was too familiar. And you see, when people in charge think you're gettin' too near to being like them, it scares them. I was too young to know your grandfather. Poppas are different than mommas. If poppas don't show you they love you, it's because it's not their job to show you. They show you by providin' for the family. Even when your grandfather died, he left me and your gram taken care of. But I tell you, poppas love their daughters, like mommas love their sons.

"I know you're a girl. You're just what your poppa needs. Once he sets eyes on you, he won't let her take you. You'll see. He'll see. We'll all see.

"It's really coming down, isn't it? That tub is about full. It'll be put to good use. One day, your gram was washin' my hair—she would always wash it with 'God's tears' because that water was from heaven and still soft. She said that it was the earth and its ways that made water hard. While she was washin' my hair, I asked her if she missed my poppa. She said she did. But God had always made it so that women outlived men. That way women could have time to be by themselves—a time to be in the world without a reason bein' placed upon it. That women had so many faces: a face for their husband, a face for their children, a face for strangers; only when they were alone could they find that face that suited just them. And if the woman happened to die before the man, that time alone would show him her worth.

"Soap got in my eyes and she thought I was cryin' because of what she was sayin'. She said that I'd understand one day, that missin' someone is a part of lovin' someone. But to stop the livin' for the dead was to spit at God's feet. I wish she was here today. She'd enjoy the rain. It's really comin' down. That's God's tears, li'l Lisa.

"Lorda be, look at that tub. It almost reminds me of church and when somebody is getting baptized; the congregation sings, 'Take me to the water. Take me to the water. Take me to the water to be baptized.' Maybe I should wash my hair; your auntie and uncle will be here before long. I want to be able to hold my head up. That's the way your gram would want it."

Momma got up and walked to the tub and squatted down; as she did, the letter that Ida Mae had sent her slipped out of the apron pocket pressed against me, where she had placed it for safekeeping. The tub was filled to the rim, and the letter, with the weight of no more than a few drops of rain, made the water creep over the edge of the washtub, wetting Momma's swollen feet. She stood up straight and watched the letter make its way to the bottom, her name on the envelope becoming a blur. There was no need in saving it now. It was where it belonged, with tears of joy. God's tears.

We're expecting Auntie Clariece and Uncle James at any moment. Poppa keeps looking out the screen door, looking for the headlights that soon will make the drops of rain glow as the wind whirls behind the car. Every now and then, Momma says something just to fill the quiet. Though it has been raining all day, in the house, it feels like the calm before a storm.

Momma takes a minute to sit down. I've been moving quite a bit today. I've proved that though you can love someone, you can hurt them as well. Every time I'd move, Momma would rub me, saying, "You're goin' to be a fighter. I can tell that already," and then I'd kick again. I couldn't help it.

"It doesn't look like the rain's goin' to slack up any, J. T.," says Momma. "The road may just be too bad for them to get here." Since Poppa had come back from Teacake's, he hadn't said a word. It was like he was trying to stay out of everybody's way. Momma had pressed his best clothes, and he had even shaved. It surprised everybody, because he hadn't shaved since he'd gotten laid off, and the pepper-colored scruff had seasoned his face. When he came out from the bathroom, everybody's eyes near about popped out. Momma told him he looked handsome; she was pleased to say it.

"Here comes the car," says Junior, standing at the screen door. He doesn't move away from it. He stands there, watching the car moving closer to the house. Poppa doesn't move either. You can see the sweat relaxing underneath Poppa's arms, and the humidity of this night in May is only partially to blame.

"Junior, don't just stand there. Go on out and greet your auntie and uncle," says Momma as she goes to the mirror and takes a quick last look, making sure the right face is in place. "J. T.? J. T., it's gonna be fine. It's gonna be fine."

"Mercy me. It's rainin' cats and dogs out there," says Auntie, entering through the screen door. "I'm almost sure I saw Noah down the road collectin' animals. Looks to me like he missed a few."

"Junior, take their coats," says Momma. Poppa hasn't said anything. He just stands there, like he wants to move but he's weary of making the wrong one.

"Anna, it's so good to see you. It's been too long. When was it . . . ?"

"Last—"

"Christmas, I believe it was. That's just too, too long to be away from kinfolk, and look at these here boys. Come on over here and give your Auntie Clariece a hug. But not too hard, though. The rain is makin' my arthritis act up."

One by one, the boys hug her. How fine is the line between wanting and having to do something?

"Joseph, it's good to see you," says Uncle James, shaking Poppa's hand. "Pardon the glove—"

"James and them gloves," says Auntie Clariece, cutting Uncle off. "No matter the temperature, he wears them gloves. Calls them his drivin' gloves, like all the peoples up north."

". . . So nice of y'all to let us stop in," says Uncle James. "We've been up since early mawnin' and this little stopover will do us a wealth of good. Joe, boy, I tell you, you can't begin to imagine what it's

like to be stuck in the car with that sister of yourn
for too long a time."

"We glad to have you . . ."

"Li'l Man, you don't have no hug for your big
sister? Now, I know you ain't too grown to give
your own sister a hug."

Poppa walks to her and they hug, if you want to
call it that. It's more like new dance partners meeting for the first time. They know the steps, but their
rhythms don't come together. The hug lasts a blink,
and in the next breath, Auntie Clariece is off again.

"Anna, what is that smellin' so downright good
up in here? You are a miracle worker, I tell you.
And look at Li'l Man, lookin' all sweet in his Sun-
day-go-to-meetin' clothes. I know you must've
picked them out for him. He ain't never been one
for clothes. A ragamuffin, if anythin'. Now, I was
the clotheshorse of the family. Now, James—see,
James got this here suit tailored by this man from
up north when we was up there for the national
choir convention. To hear those chilren sangin' for
the Lawd is the most beautiful thang in the world.
A joyful noise indeed. And when James got up to
preach, the collection plate runneth over. Set the
record for the convention, and that don't even in-
clude the tithes . . . It amazes me that with all these
boys around here, you can still keep a steady
house—"

"That's more than I can say for you," says Uncle
James, stopping her momentum with his laughter.

"Ain't that right, Joe?" Poppa nods and Auntie Cla-riece looks at him, then goes on.

"Oh, James is always goin' on at me, about one thing or the other. But he knows it ain't easy bein' a preacher's wife. People look at me in a certain way. They *suspect* me to be a certain way and have certain things. They pro'bly watches me more than they do him. You should have seen the women today at that revival down in Manville. Chile, when they wasn't eyein' James, they was eyein' my hat, wishin' they could have both." Her hat was red with a black crow's feather atop it, high as it was wide. You couldn't help but eye it.

"Well, you in the house now, so why don't you rest your hat?"

"Now, James, if my hat is good enough to wear in the house of the Lawd, then it's certainly good enough to wear in my brother's. Now, what was I . . . ? Oh. When I walked in that church, they knew I was the preacher's wife. And God was on my side, 'cuz not a drop of rain hit that hat, and I thanked Him dearly for it."

"They knew you were the preacher's wife 'cuz you kept sayin' to them, 'Well, my husband, the Reverend James Caldwell, this, and my husband, the Reverend James Caldwell, that.' That's how they knew you were the preacher's wife. I tell you, Jo-seph, your sister recites so much I barely get a word in edgewise, and I'm the one up in the pulpit. I try and tell her there's a difference between a joyful noise and just plain noise, but she can't seem to decipher," says Uncle James, giving Poppa a friendly punch and filling the house with laughter, a sound that had been a stranger to the walls of our home lately. Auntie laughs right along with him as her eyes look at everybody to see what they're thinking. She always seemed different when Uncle James was there. Now, she's being, if not nice, at least decent. She still is the bearer of conversation, but that's fine because it keeps everyone else from having to say anything, though thoughts and minds are at work.

"Well, whatever the reason, I'm sure the sermon was a good one," says Momma. "Supper'll be ready shortly. Can I get y'all anythin' to drink while you wait?"

"Beggin' your pardon, Anna, but I regret I'm goin' to have to pass on what I'm sure will be a delicious supper. I told the Reverend Ferguson that I would stop in and pay tribute while I was in the area. But I'm sure Clariece will tell me all about it," says Uncle James. He had a way about him: he could probably spit on you and you still would think it was the most beautiful thing that had ever happened to you.

"You see how it is bein' married to a preacher. Their work is never done. Always on the go. Go, go, go. And it's the preacher's wife gets left to be *hospital*. Now James, don't be too long. With this weather as it is, we should make ace and get back on the road for home before it's too late," says Auntie, straightening Uncle's tie and wiping away at his suit jacket even though not a speck was to be found.

"Well, I'm sorry you won't be stayin', James," says Momma, helping him with his coat. Uncle may truly be sorry for having to leave, but not more so about it than Momma is.

"Next time, I promise. 'Sides, from the looks of you, we just may be seein' more of you real soon. You just shootin' out."

Uncle pats Momma's belly and I kick, but Momma doesn't show it. She bites through her friendly smile. "I guess so. Let me show you out." Momma walks Uncle out to the porch and softly closes the screen door behind them. "James."

"Yes?"

I can feel a change around me and in Momma. I almost feel as if at any moment I'll burst. I kick again almost in time with the heartbeat that makes the word *nothing* sadly come out of Momma's mouth.

"Anna, is ever'thang awright?"

"Fine, James. Ever'thin' is fine."

Uncle comes close to us and takes Momma's hand in his gloved ones. He rubs hers as he speaks. "Well, you know if you need anythang, you can just let me know. I 'preciate what you doin' for us. Both me and Clariece realize that you don't have to do what you doin', but with the misfortunes we've had, it does mean a great deal to the both of us. I just wanted to let you know that we 'preciate you thinkin' of us in this matter." Uncle looks in Momma's eyes like he's looking for a verse in the scripture that he knows he's seen but can't place. "You sure you're fine with this arrangement?"

"In all honesty, James, I . . ."

"Anna, deah. I believe somethin's burnin'," says Auntie, looking through the screen door. "James, you're still out here? I thought you'd gone. You better be runnin' along now. Reverend Ferguson is bound to be waitin'. The Lawd's work can't be put on hold. There's sinners to save."

"I better check on the food." Momma slides her hand from Uncle's. Uncle smiles at Momma and puts on his hat before walking toward the car. The farther he walks away from the house, the harder the rain seems to come down, each drop covering the next until he can no longer be seen.

The lights from the car come on, lighting up the porch. Auntie opens the screen door wide while standing to the side, allowing her arm to hold it open. Momma watches the car drive away, then watches as Auntie waves good-bye to Uncle James with her other arm. When we are safe in the house, the only noise to be heard is that of the rain hitting the tin roof and the hinge on the screen door releasing its tension, only to provide more tension with its slam.

... A tornado came through. It took the Dawsons' place, down the way. We could see the twister from the house. J. T. put us all in the bathroom and stood at the door like he could fight it off. I think he thought he could. Deep down, I know he'd try if he had to. But in the end, the tornado took another course, sparing us, this time . . .

7

Today turned to July and Momma says she's 'most certain that I'm due any time now. Since Uncle and Auntie's visit, Momma has been having a rough time of it; making matters worse, Poppa told her this morning that Auntie would be coming tomorrow to stay with us until I was born. He said that was what she wanted to do, and he thought it would be a good idea because Momma had been slowing down lately and some help around the house would do her good. Momma told me that that kind of help she could live without.

A week or so ago another letter came from Ida Mae.

Dear Precious:
  I've moved from Hitsville, U.S.A., to Chicago, the Windy City, 'cuz they said it's better, but I

don't see nary a difference. Believe it or not, I had more fun in the ol' *M, i*, crooked letter, crooked letter, *i*, crooked letter, crooked letter, *i*, humpback, humpback, *i*.

They calls it Chi-town, but you know there ain't a shy bone in my body. Good thang, too, 'cuz I'm workin' in a club. I walk 'round takin' drink orders, drankin' two for ever' one I serve. They all drinks bourbon, so the latest drink up north is from the South. It's a nice club, though, and you got to dress up real nicelike, better than for church. You know I loves to dress. The womens fight up in here more than the menfolk. Always over a man. If you could see these grown women rollin' 'round on the floor. They know to stay out of my way. Most of 'em scared of me. I don't know why (smile).

I hope you sittin' down. Now, don't have a heart attack, but I'm comin' down there. Not to stay, just a visit for the Fourth, so if that heathen'll let you, we can go to the fireworks together—if you ain't still scared of it poppin' in your hand.

I cain't wait to tell you all the stories. Maybe we can go to the creek and stick our legs in like ol' times. You can't do that up here. I hear tell of the Great Lakes, but ain't a damn thang great 'bout 'em as far as I can see. Even the fish is— are (smile)—lookin' to move.

If you didn't sit down, you really better sit

down now, so you can jump up again. Believe it or not, I met me a man I've taken a likin' to. He a musician in the club. Treats me real nice. That's 'cuz he knows what's good for him. I never thought I'd see the day someone 'sides you could tame me, but this here man has. His name is John Worth of the Alabama Worths. Damn shame I had to come up here to find a decent man when he was in my back yard all the whiles. He plays the sax. The man can blow. But that's a story I can only tell you when I sees you.

For now, I better get to work or I ain't gonna be goin' nowhere. See you on the Fourth.
Love,
Ida Mae

That letter has kept Momma going. I haven't been making it any easier. I keep getting bigger and in need of more. Momma is already giving so much.

I can now say I do know the difference between laughing and crying; only one has been going on since Auntie left from her last visit. Hearing this morning of her return didn't bring great joy, for anybody.

During their last visit, when Uncle James left to go meet Reverend Ferguson, Auntie became the Auntie that we knew of that Christmas past. When the food was on the table, she complained. If this was the way I was being "nourished," she said, then she wasn't sure she wanted me. Junior stood up from the table like he was going to throw it over, but Momma gave him the same look she gave him that night on the porch when he swore in front of her. He left the table and Auntie told Poppa to make him come back and sit down. Poppa said it, but Junior didn't mind him. Junior's eye had long since healed, and he wasn't afraid of what a rematch might bring.

"It's plain to see, Li'l Man, that you ain't the man of this house. These chilren just runs all over you. I can't rightly tell who the chilren is here. And these two over here, lookin' like Satan on earth. Don't you be eyein' me. I'll slap the taste right out of your mouth—the both of you," she said, pointing her crooked finger at the twins.

"Momma says it's not polite to point," said Leo.

Auntie got up from her chair—Poppa's chair—and started toward them. Both Leo and Leon stood, too.

"Li'l Man? Is that what you're teachin' these here chilren? Is that what? You sit here while they disrespect me that way? Like I don't even matter. Well, I think maybe one of you should come and live with me for a spell. I bet the separation would change some thangs. That and a nice swat on those spoilt bottoms ever' now and again would wash the sass right out of those mouths. That and some soap."

Momma told Leo and Leon to go into the living room and keep Junior company, after which Edward and Leselle asked to be excused, too. Auntie laughed. Poppa sat there like he wanted to ask permission to leave the table, also, but was afraid of what the answer might prove to be.

"Well, all I know, Li'l Man, is you must be makin' a fortune down at the mill to let all this good food go to waste," said Auntie, going back to her chair—Poppa's chair. "If these were my chilren, they would eat ever'thang I put on their plates and be glad to do it. Just like Ma Dear used to make us do. It shouldn't be your place to work hard to bring home good money and let this one here waste it. We all aren't able to have ever'thang given to us. As long as you been workin' at that lumber mill, you of all people should know money don't grow on trees."

Auntie looked away from Poppa, toward Momma sitting next to her. She wiped the corners of her mouth with her napkin and threw it over her plate, pushing it away. Then she put her elbows on the table and placed her hands together to rest her chins upon.

"But I s'pose you pro'bly can afford it. 'Course, you ain't no preacher or nothin', but you been at the mill some time. I saw you was wearin' your Sunday's best when I came in. I s'pose you work in an office now and leave the grunt work for Junior. He's gotten so big, a man hisself. He'll be wantin' to settle down soon. I tell you, when I stand next to him, I feel like his sister. That's 'cuz my age don't show—lookin' younger ever'day.

"Anna, deah. It's just plain bad manners to leave a empty plate in front of your guest. I put my napkin on the plate. When a person does that, that means they finished. I know y'all don't get out that much, but do try and remember that for future *preference*. See, I have to know these thangs. As I said, a preacher's wife's job is never done."

When Poppa got a word in, he finally found the nerve to tell her he didn't work at the mill anymore. She was fit to be tied. The veins surfaced on her forehead, forking like that of the mighty river so often spoken of, as she scolded him in front of the entire household. Momma stopped her by taking the attention off Poppa and placing it upon herself.

"You want some more coffee, Clariece?"

"Did I ask you for more coffee? My word! Ever'time I come to this Godforsaken house, I come with a clear head and leave with a headache! I s'pose it would be too much to ask for an Anacin."

"I'll get you one," said Poppa, finally moving from the table.

"I need more than one. And don't put your hands all over 'em. I don't want none of your germs touchin' 'em. Li'l Man? Li'l Man, you hear me? I said don't . . ."

"He heard you," said Momma. She said it where only Auntie could hear. And for the first time since she had arrived, Auntie was silent and puzzlement made her squint as if her eyes and ears were playing tricks on her.

When Poppa came back with the aspirin, Auntie and Momma were still staring at one another. Momma left the two alone and went to check on the boys.

"If you'll excuse me, I'm goin' to see about my chilren."

"Seems to me you're a li'l too late for that, but good, go check on them. It'll give me and Li'l Man here a chance to catch up, talk over a few thangs."

Uncle James came back to pick up Auntie Clariece in a couple of hours, but he didn't come in. He blew the car horn and Auntie put on her coat and made her way to the car, with everybody standing at the door watching. The walk was a bit muddy, and with every step that Auntie made, an imprint was left in the drenched earth. The rain, falling behind her, quickly filled her steps, drowning each print until every trace of her disappeared.

"I wish she would slip and fall," said Leon, and everybody laughed for a moment—everybody except for Poppa.

"That ain't no way to talk about your Ma Dear, boy."

"But, Poppa, that ain't my—"

"Leon, all you boys, it's late, go get ready for bed," said Momma.

Junior took them all away. When Uncle James blew the horn to signal farewell, Poppa's hand, as

if connected by a cord to the sound, went up and
waved to Auntie Clariece. It wasn't a "good-bye"
wave—just " 'bye." Momma started rubbing the
back of his shirt, and like the rain that reigned over
that day, it, too, was wet.

> ... I read your letter to li'l Lisa. I know she
> could feel the joy it brought me. I know that
> sounds crazy, but I talk to her like she could
> answer me. . . .
> I'd been wishing for a letter from you, and that
> wish came true. That gives me hope. The moon
> has always done right by me, for even the moon
> must wish upon the first star, because it takes so
> much strength to wish upon yourself . . .

Auntie's visit stayed in our house, keeping joy
away like the smell of burning sulfur used to keep
mosquitoes and snakes away.

Junior was made shift leader at the mill and got
a higher wage, so he and Poppa had words 'most
every day. Words were pretty much all they *could*
have these days because Junior had had a "growing
spurt" and was big as Poppa—stronger, too. The
plant kept his body firm, while Poppa's had begun
to soften. It couldn't really be called baby fat, but
all the same, that's what Momma called it during
those few playful moments between the two.

Corn liquor brought the gruff back to Poppa's
face, and when he wasn't at the Rusty Nail or at

Teacake's, he'd just sit on the porch in his rocker. Most of the boys stayed away from him because of his temper. Everybody did their best to make sure all the chores were done before needed so that nothing would set him off again.

... If you get married, you have to do it down here, being he's from this area, too. We'll have a big wedding. I can't wait to meet this sax man. But if he can keep up with you, he must be okay.

I know you've probably made other friends, but I hope I can be your first maid. Don't worry, I won't be able to wear white either. The twins can carry the rings. I'm just getting all ahead of myself. But I've not been to a wedding since my own. Somedays it's like it was yesterday; other days . . .

Anna and Joseph's wedding was the best day of Anna's life. The service at the church was a blur because she was so happy and all the blood rushed to her head. It was what was considered—by the folks that were there—a "big weddin'." Missus Anderson felt that her only daughter deserved it and believed it was the way Mr. Anderson would have wanted it. Ida Mae stood up for Anna; Teacake, for Joseph. There were three flower girls, and a li'l boy and girl carried the rings up to the front of the church when the time came for the passing of the wedding bands.

Anna and Joseph passed rings. Anna remembered the night her mother gave the rings to her. They had been passed on for years and years, from way back over the "Sea of Darkness." Anna remembered that she was so pleased to now give them to her daughter and her husband. Along with the house at the end of their property, Missus Anderson also offered, as a wedding gift, to have the bands adjusted to size if need be. Only Joseph's needed adjusting. Having worked in the mill for so long, his knuckles were bigger, different from any of the men's in Anna's family, and therefore it couldn't be so easily slid into place.

The reception was said to be a howl. Everybody came over to the house Missus Anderson gave Anna—and Joseph—even Clariece, who everybody looked at when the preacher said speak now or forever hold your peace. She was just Clariece back then, not a "preacher's wife."

Everybody was feeling happy. The men huddled in their corner and the women in theirs, each group speaking only of the other. All the women commented on Anna's dress, and the men told Joseph how he was the luckiest Negro in all of Welty County. Anna's dress had a long train on it. At the service, Teacake kept stepping on it and, having

only one good leg, he would almost slip and fall.
He'd apologize every time, and every time Missus
Anderson would give him a look and say, "Careful,
Lawrence, that's an heirloom." To which Teacake
said that the air couldn't be any better for a wed-
ding than it was.

Everyone seemed to be at the reception, even
folks that nobody seemed to know. But it's said that
that goes along with a big wedding. "The more the
merrier." There was more than enough food. Anna
said there was more food than for a "funeral on a
Sunday." The food had been placed on the kitchen
table and on the counters; every spot was covered
with something homemade.

Laughter filled the house and overflowed to the
front and back porch, baptizing Anna and Joseph's
new home. When there was a loud noise in the living room, everybody turned their attention to it. It
was Teacake taking the floor.

"As the best man, and the worst man . . ."

Joseph yelled out, "Well, ya half right."

Everybody laughed.

"As the best man, I'd like to pose a toast to my
good friend, Joseph: boy, I hope you know what
you doin'."

Missus Anderson said, "He'd better."

Everybody laughed.

Ida Mae raised her glass. "To all the men in the world: just remember, ever' dog has his day."

Teacake said, "Well, if anybody should know 'bout dogs, it's you."

Everybody laughed.

"That may be, but even dogs get tired of bein' messed wit and will bite." Ida Mae growled.

Everybody laughed.

Joseph walked over to where Ida Mae and Anna were standing and said, "You always gotta have the last word, don'tcha?" Ida Mae just smiled. That was enough. When the crowd quieted from her speech, Joseph took the floor.

"To my friends here with me today, Porkchop, Popcorn, Neckbone, Cornbread, Teacake . . ."

Ida Mae said, "Are those friends or a five-course meal?"

More laughter.

Anna whispered, "Ah, Ida Mae."

" 'Ah, Ida Mae' nothin'. All of 'em just boys in men's clothin'."

". . . Boys, I wish I could share this feelin' witcha. But I don't think Anna's momma would 'low it."

Everybody laughed.

Missus Anderson stood up. "To my beautiful daughter . . ."

Teacake said, "You half right."

"Don't make me have to set your leg on fire, Law-rence," snapped Missus Anderson.

"Though I hate to let you loose, my dear daugh-ter, I gladly set you free."

At the end of Missus Anderson's toast, Auntie Clariece stood and said, "Li'l Man, I wish Ma Dear was here to see this."

Something about her phrasing took away the joy-ous feeling of the day from the room. Anna never got to say her toast. To dispell the awkward air, all she managed to get out was "I hope everyone's hun-gry, because there's enough food in here to feed Africa."

Everybody laughed. But this time the laughter came more as something to do when what to do was so unclear.

The day after Auntie left, Momma and I went for a long walk before supper. The softness of the earth underfoot was the only evidence that rain had stormed through the day before. The days lingered into night this time of year, and sunset was still a while away.

We walked through the cornfield, for what to me seemed like forever. Momma stopped several times to catch her breath. She often complained about her back, never out loud, but I heard her all the same. When we came out of the fields, we walked a bit longer and then came out on a trail. Down that road there was a big house, bigger than ours. We walked to the house but didn't go in. The paint had started to curl off the wood and the curtains in the windows had been stained by years of intruding sunlight. We walked around the house to the back yard, where two ropes were hanging from the branch on an old pecan tree. Below the ropes, on the ground, were the remains of a flat piece of wood.

"You see this, li'l Lisa?" Momma said to me as if she had me by the hand and I could answer. "This used to be my swing. Your gram used to come out here and push me, and I would scream like a crazy person. The higher she'd push me, the louder I'd scream. Then one day when we were in the kitchen, I didn't have anythin' to do, so I asked her to come push me. She said that she wouldn't because I had to learn how to do it myself, that I was big enough to swing myself.

"Well, I had never done it before and didn't think I could. But I came out here, and the swing was too far off the ground for me to sit in. Your gram had always picked me up and put me in the seat, makin' sure I had my balance before she began to push. But that day, I took these ropes, one in each hand, and with all my strength, I pulled myself up on that swing. I started to rock back and forth, makin' my weight shift—just like it does when I bend down with you and you shift with me. But the swing wouldn't go. I screamed for my momma to come out the house and push me, but she didn't answer. I was so frustrated, but I just kept on tryin'.

"Before long, I was swingin' myself, and I got up real high, almost even with the branch where the ropes were tied. I could feel the slack in the rope. The nearer I got to that branch, the more slack there'd be. Then on the way back down, it would tighten. I'd swing my legs under me, then kick them out for another go, fear and excitement fillin' ever' inch of my body.

"And you know what, li'l Lisa? I was much higher than your gram had ever pushed me, but I didn't scream. Not once did I scream. The fear soon found its way from me, leavin' only excitement. I knew I'd done it. Sometimes I would even jump off the swing while it was at its highest point and go flyin' through the air, each time going farther and farther out. When I got real good at it, I'd take a stick or a piece of bark, a rock, anything I could find, to mark where it was I'd landed. Then I'd run back and climb on that swing and jump out again, settin' a new world's record.

"One time I looked at the kitchen window right over there. And there she was, lookin' all worried because I was goin' too high. She never came out to say anythin', but she was always watchin'."

Momma held those two ropes in her hand, and the way she was telling it, I felt as if we were both on that swing, swinging just like she used to. With her foot, she moved the piece of wood. Nature had

had its way, though, and at the touch of her foot, it was now nothing more than just splintered memories.

We began to walk away from the house, and then Momma stopped; she slowly kneeled down. To those unfamiliar, this looked like any other piece of grass, but this was where Gram and Papa were buried. There was no headstone to say it; you just had to know. We knelt there for some time, and the only thing Momma said was "The swing's broken, Momma."

When we got up, Momma's dress was wet where the moisture from the earth had clung to the fabric; signs of things past. Again, we walked back by the swing, that house. Momma stopped and took a long look. The moon and the sun both seemed in arm's reach, each providing a different light, but it was the straightness of the rows of corn that led our way. As we walked deeper into the field, the day's sun sank into each golden stalk and it was warm. But the nearer we got to the house, the temperature seemed to drop. I was now kicking on a regular basis, and each time I was sorry for the discomfort it would bring Momma.

The house was in sight, but it wasn't that that made Momma quicken her stride. There was a scream. Like any animal, you know the scream of your offspring. Momma ran onto the back porch and through the door, which slammed behind her, causing the rainwater in the washtub to ripple, waking it from rest. The screams grew louder, and when Momma got to the living room, she saw things were thrown all about the place and Poppa had a strop in his hand. Leon was bent down with his head between Poppa's legs. On the downswing of the strop, Momma grabbed Poppa's arm. In anger, he lifted his other hand over his shoulder as if he was going to hit her, but she held a steady eye and his hand found its way back to his side.

The strop fell out of his hand and he let Leon go. Leon ran away to the other boys. Momma still had Poppa's arm when he fell to the ground and began to cry, just as he had done the night of his dream. And again, the same words came from his mouth: "I'm sorry, Anna. I'm so sorry." Momma picked him up and took him to the room in order to put him to bed. Again the smell of liquor made her sick, but this time the sickness wasn't in her stomach.

When Poppa was settled in the room, Momma came out and began to pick up the mess. The end table had been knocked over. And there, on the floor next to it, was the gray ceramic elephant, showing its hollow insides. Momma had once told me she hoped she'd live to see the day when she could pass that elephant on to me. But that would never come to pass. It seemed all good luck was shattered.

Because of Junior's promotion, he got off work later, but when he came home, Momma was still picking up the pieces. It took the remaining strength in Momma's body to keep him from going in and waking Poppa.

"How much of this can you take, Momma?" said Junior, looking at her tenderly, and standing in the frame of a man. "How much more?"

Momma had no answer.

The day before Ida Mae left for up north, Anna went over to see her one last time. When Anna's mother had passed on, Ida Mae had been her strength, but now she, too, was leaving.

"I'm surprised that dog of a husband a yourn let you come over," said Ida Mae, putting on the finishing touches of her makeup.

"Ida Mae, as long as I've known you, you've never had a kind word for Joseph. He's not that bad, you know," said Anna, thumbing through Ida Mae's "magic potions."

"Try on this shade. You'd look nice with this."

"No, I'd better not. I'm gonna have to get home directly. Joseph went over to Teacake's to play horseshoes. He should be back soon."

"Girl, sit down in this chair, and be quiet for a minute. Damn. Ever since you married that bow-legged creature, you always got some excuse why you can't do somethin' or somethin' else. Now, I said this shade would look good on you, and you gonna at least give me the satisfaction of lettin' me

see it on you." Ida Mae put the lipstick on Anna. "There. That looks nice. Sho do. Here. Now put on this hat." Ida Mae put a green pill hat with a red feather on Anna's head. That hat had been Ida Mae's prize possession. She had ordered it through a mail-order catalog from Rosenblum's, a store up north—the place she'd soon be off to.

"G'on girl! Look atcha. You look good enough to eat. Green suits you."

"But not as pretty as you," said Anna, looking at herself in the mirror.

"I don't ever wanna hear you talk like that. Hear? You are the most beautiful person I know. Always have been, and ever'body knows it. You don't need no hat or no lipstick to make you beautiful, you hear? You've got somethin' that don't need to be made up, and don't you forget it. Don't you ever forget it."

Ida Mae was serious. All of her years of joking had come to this. She didn't say it in a way that was off the cuff. It came out like bullets hitting tin cans perched on a fencepost. She meant it, and in that moment, she was more than beautiful, too.

"Lawd. Look at you, Anna. My precious. I wish that I was nearly as . . ." And as was custom for her, she dropped her serious tone and smiled through it. "Now, of course, I ain't somethin' to throw out as slop to pigs my own self. But as we

all know, black don't crack." Ida Mae laughed and she and Anna giggled like they were little girls jumping in Anna's bed at Missus Anderson's.

"Listen, why don't you come out with me to the Nail tonight? Turn some heads. Shake the cricks out of a few of those tired ol' necks."

"No, I can't. Junior is lookin' after Edward and Leselle and I told him I wouldn't be long. With three children, I barely have time to pee without one of them being there. Anyway, what would it look like for a pregnant woman tippin' up into a juke joint? People would talk. It doesn't even look like you're packed yet. Your train leaves first thing in the mornin'. You shouldn't be goin' out yourself."

"Precious, this is the night I been waitin' for all my life. Talk is what I'm after, 'cuz that's sho all they gonna get tonight. You don't know how I've dreamed about it. Oh yes, I am sho goin' out and strut my stuff for these countrified people one last time. I want them to remember Ida Mae Ramsey. And remember they will! I'll pack in the mornin', but there are a few thangs I want to get off my chest before I go, and the Nail is just the place to do it."

"Just mind what you say. You never know. You might have to come back down here for whatever reason. I mean, if things don't work out."

"Oh, Anna, I love you wit all my heart. But sometimes don't you wanna just say the hell with it and do somethin' whether you'll regret it or not?"

"Sometimes I do. But that's what dreamin' is for. In my dreams, I can do all the things that I want to and nobody gets hurt or disappointed."

"Hurt comes in different ways."

"I know, but you remember my momma always sayin' to us not to burn our bridges."

"Well, Missus Anderson ain't here now, so I give you permission to do somethin' crazy. Anyhow, I believe that there comes a day when you have to burn your bridges just to make sure you can still swim."

"What if you can't?"

"Then you either learn real fastlike or you drown. And I don't plan on drownin' no time soon."

"I'm going to miss you." Anna grabbed Ida Mae and held on tight. Anna knew her hold was not enough to make Ida Mae stay, and her love for her was too powerful to ever think of wanting her to.

"Now don't you go doin' this to me. Don't you dare start cryin'. If you do, then you know I will, too. Then my makeup'll start runnin', messin' up this work a art." They both laughed and cried and held each other.

"You sure you won't come out and play with me tonight?"

"Yes. I don't think I'd be much fun."

"So. This is good-bye then?" said Ida Mae, looking at Anna like a mother looking at her child.

"I guess it is."

"Why don't you just keep this lipstick? It looks good. Never know when you might need it."

"You've already given me so much."

"Girl, I haven't given you nothin' in a long time."

"Oh, yes you have." Anna looked at Ida Mae as if it would be for the last time—childhood friends going their separate ways. Anna didn't know if the pain she felt was due to Ida Mae leaving or the fact that she could leave. "Thank you. I'll wear it well."

"I'm sho you will. Now listen, I want you to be careful, you hear. Don't let that man of yourn get to you. I'd hate to have to come back down here jus' to give him a good ol'-fashion' ass-whuppin'."

"Don't you worry about that. You just take care of yourself up there. It's different."

"I will. And stop talkin' like I'm dead or somethin'. It's bad luck. I'm gonna come back and see you. And when that husband of yourn kicks the bucket, we'll go and live in your momma's old house and grow old together."

They hugged one last time, then Anna started for the door.

"Ida Mae?"

"Yes, precious?"

"Do you really think I'm beautiful?"

"As a night full of stars."

Anna walked out and started back home. When she got there, Joseph had already made it back. In anticipation, she had prepared an explanation, but before the words could come from her mouth, he looked at her and said, "Look at you. Don't you look nice?"

"Why, thank you, J. T. Thank you."

Momma is convinced that I'm due any day now. When Leselle asked how she knew, Momma just said, "A woman knows these things."

I've been hungry, really hungry. Momma says that she shouldn't eat so near to when I'm expected. Even with the news of Auntie Clariece coming to-morrow, Momma refused to be discouraged. Two things made this so. One was that Ida Mae would soon be here. The other was with Auntie Clariece's arrival, our family would, once again, be back together.

It's safe to say the past weeks have been trying times. Auntie Clariece had made a suggestion on her last visit that, at the time, seemed only that; but she had actually separated the twins.

One day, Poppa sent Momma to the market and said he would watch the boys, an offer not often made. When Momma returned, she found Poppa sitting in his rocker, silent. She found Leo in the bedroom. Edward and Leselle were leaning over him. Leo's eyes were red, as red as Poppa's, but from tears, not cheap wine. He came running at Momma.

"She took him!"

"What, Leo? Stop cryin' and speak up, honey. What's wrong?"

"She . . . she . . ."

"Auntie came and took Leon. She dragged him to her car and drove away," said Edward. "We tried to stop her, but Poppa told us to go back in the house. We tried, Momma. We did."

"Leon? Leon? Okay, boys, this isn't funny. All right. Come on out." Momma walked out to the porch, where Poppa was still sitting.

"Joseph . . ."

"He wit Clariece. She said it would be good to have a chile for a while 'fo' they baby come. She gonna keep him just for a few weeks. James gonna be in and out doin' sermons. She wanted somebody 'round the house wit her."

Poppa said it almost as if he was repeating the words to and for himself as they had been said to him. He didn't look at Momma. Momma started laughing.

"Okay, now, enough fooling. Where is Leon? He must be with Junior."

It took a few hours before Momma accepted what was being said as truth. She kept looking at the door, expecting Leon to come through it at any moment. It wasn't until Junior came in and she didn't see Leon with him that she accepted the fact that Leon was gone. As soon as Poppa told Momma what had happened, Poppa headed off; I kept kicking.

Leo has been sick ever since. He won't talk; a part of his vocabulary is gone. Edward and Leselle have been trying to make him feel better, but nothing helps. Momma can't even look at him. She never thought that she'd be happy to see Auntie Clariece, but this time she would be. The visit meant getting her child back. Though she knew it would be nothing more than a swap. Me for Leon. One child for another.

Momma went into the room to tuck in the boys, three instead of four. When she got to Leo, he was on his side. He didn't roll over. He just stared at the wall like it was alive. Momma sat—in the empty spot.

"Leon will be here tomorrow, Leo. He'll be here tomorrow. Listen, honey, I know it's been hard on you, but tomorrow, it'll be over. He'll be back with us—back in the home where he belongs. I'm sorry. I know you're mad at me now, but I want you to know that I am sorry."

Momma got up and we walked to the door.

"Momma?" Leo didn't roll over, but the words came out his mouth. "Will you stay in here till I fall asleep?"

A chill ran through Momma and, for the first time in a few weeks, she felt as if she was Momma again.

"Of course I will. You just go on and sleep. Nothin' is going to mess with you. Just go on and sleep. I'll be right here."

We walked back to the bed and sat in the spot, filling the void of where Leon would normally be, and after tomorrow would be again.

With Leo finally asleep, Momma went out to the porch, where Junior was sitting with his Bible.

"I haven't seen you reading that lately."

"I didn't think it would do any good. Things don't seem to be gettin' any better."

"Your gram used to say that it wasn't so much about how much you read it, but that you have faith."

"Do you have faith?"

"Well, Junior, I must say it seems like my life has been full of 'I don't knows.' For most of my life, all of my decisions have been made for me. And you trust that they're what's best. I wake up in the mornin's and the only thing I know for sure is that I'm alive."

"Is that enough? Bein' alive?"

"If you truly are, I guess it is. But there are times, many times, I don't even feel like I am. If it wasn't for this baby and you boys, I don't think I would feel alive. When I look at Leo, I think about Leon and how I'd rather die than give her my baby."

"I told the boys that Auntie was going to take the baby."

Momma looked at Junior, and her gaze went quickly from anger and surprise to at ease.

"I was in there tonight. Leo wouldn't even look at me. As I was about to walk out, he asked me to stay with him till he fell asleep. Junior? Junior, I want to thank you. You had to grow up too quickly. I realize that and I'm sorry for it. I'm sittin' out here talkin' to you about things that a mother shouldn't have to speak of with a child. I know you're not a child anymore—far from it—but still, it isn't fair to you. It's not fair to anybody and I'm sorry for that burden, too."

Junior didn't say anything. He sat there, the quiet embracing us all. When he realized Momma wasn't going to say anything, Junior told her it was all right. She smiled and nodded her head. Junior got up to go into the house.

"Junior? You mind if I hold on to that Bible for a bit?"

Junior walked over and handed it to Momma, then went into the house. The night was still; even the katydids seemed to be cooperating, providing the peace that Momma so desperately needed. She smelled the Bible, in search of a trace of Gram, then she opened it, resting it on me, and I, too, was at ease.

"What are you doing?" whispered Anna when she looked out her bedroom window. "My momma will kill you if she finds you here."

"I'll just have to risk it. I bought these flowers for you."

"You mean you stole them out of somebody's yard."

"Come down."

"You must not like breathin'. My momma's got a shotgun by her bed and she's by no means afraid of using it."

"Well, if you don't come down, then I guess I'll just have to wake her up."

"No. Okay. I'll come down. Meet me in the back yard. And be quiet about it," whispered Anna.

Anna went down that night and Joseph was all dressed up. He had given our mutt some meat—Jimmy was easily won over.

"Some guard dog you are, Jimmy, you ol' mutt," said Anna when she came down. Then to Joseph, she said, "Why are you all dressed up?"

"I figured if your momma caught me, at least I'd awready be dressed for my funeral."

"You've got that right."

"Well, don't I get no reward for comin' 'round here?"

"If you came lookin' for a reward, then you shouldn't've bothered."

"Not even a little peck?"

"Chickens peck."

"I guess I'll just have to take these here flowers back."

"Suit yourself, because I know that's exactly what you'd do with a kiss, take it back to those friends of yours. Ida Mae told me all about how y'all get down to that juke joint and just tell all of y'all's business. Well, you aren't goin' to be tellin' my business, Mr. Joseph Henry Thomas."

"Come on now. 'Sides, it was Ida Mae told me to come 'round here. She said you needed a little excitement," said Joseph, playing with the ropes of the swing.

"You need to just stop tellin' stories. Ida Mae can't stand the ground you walk on, so why would she tell you to come here?" said Anna. Joseph sat in the swing.

"How you think I knew which one was your room? You think I'd take the chance if I weren't sho? Ida Mae told me you liked me. She said she didn't know why, but that you did. So I'm here to seal it."

" 'Seal it?' " said Anna teasingly, getting up in his lap on that swing that she had outgrown years ago.

"Seal it with a kiss."

Joseph pushed his legs out and the swing set sail. The evening was so pleasing to Anna, and Joseph

was as sweet. And just as they sealed their relationship, the piece of wood that held them up slid
through the ropes, their weight proving too heavy.
They both fell to the ground. Anna screamed. In a
blink of an eye, a light came on in the house. Joseph
took off so fast that even a double barrel wouldn't
be able to catch him. Missus Anderson came out
and found her daughter on the ground.

"The swing is broken, Momma."

"Yes, I see. Come on in the house; it's late."

Anna got up from the ground and started toward
the house when Missus Anderson said, "Don't forget your flowers."

When Anna saw Ida Mae the next day, she tried
to act like she was mad with her for telling Joseph
how much she liked him. The glow on her face
made Ida Mae know otherwise.

"People need a little push to get things going,"
said Ida Mae. "Just call me the engine to your
caboose."

<u>8</u>

... I'm dropping low, Ida Mae. I'm dropping low.

I sit here wondering if I'm the only one. Am I going to be looked at by those who hear what can't be kept a secret? Other women always say what they will and won't put up with, but that's easy to say, until the situation is pulling on your dress.

I refuse to believe that in this great big world, I'm the only one going through this. Still, I can truly say I hope I am . . .

I am dropping low and kicking as I do. Momma says I'm about ready to grace this place with my presence. We're up early; everybody else is still sleeping, except for Leo. He's been sitting at the door since he got up—watching, waiting.

Momma had been watching and waiting, too. The fireworks are two days away and Ida Mae swore she'd be here in time. It has all come down to a matter of time. Doesn't it always?

"Leo, I don't think they are comin' till the afternoon. Come on and spend some time with Momma before ever'body gets up." Leo stands up, hesitation shadowing his steps as he comes into the kitchen with us.

"Uh!" says Momma, grabbing at her midsection.

"Momma, you okay?"

"Yes, I'm fine. It's your li'l sister knockin' at the door."

"She ain't gonna be my li'l sister. Junior told us that Auntie Clariece is gonna take her, just like she took Leon."

"But Leo, she's your sister now."

"But she ain't born yet."

Momma picks up the dishrag and looks at Leo. We walk over to him and Momma reaches for his hand. She places his hand over her stomach, waiting for me to kick. I more than oblige, grasping for any extra room, room that doesn't seem to exist. When I kick, Leo lights up and hope comes back into his eyes and there's no discomfort for anyone; at least for a moment.

"See there? She's there."

"But not for long."

Hearing that brings a change in Momma, demanding her to sit. At any time I could be born, and what has been nothing more than a name in her mind will soon become real—as real as Auntie Clariece.

"Eat your breakfast, Leo. Your brother will be here soon."

"Hello?" Follows a knock at the door. "Y'all up in there?" We all get up from the table and run to the door.

"Oh, Teacake. It's you."

"Good mawnin' to you, too, Anna."

"No, I'm sorry, Teacake. Come on in. It's just we're expectin' someone. Leo, honey, go on and finish your breakfast."

"Yeah, last night at the Nail, Joe was tyin' one on, the way he always do when he 'bout to get a visit from the 'preacher's wife.' I s'pose he's still sleepin' it off."

"Yes. He should be up directly. Feel free to stay and wait if you like."

"Yeah. I think I will," says Teacake, taking a seat on the couch.

"Can I offer you anythin'?"

"Nah, Anna. That's awright. I don't want to be no trouble."

"It's no trouble at—"

"Well, den, a cup of coffee'd be right nice."

"All right, Teacake," says Momma, laughing. "How'd you like it?"

"I like it light."

Momma fixes the cup of coffee and brings it to him.

"That light enough for you?"

"Just right. This is the color I like my womens, too," says Teacake. Leo comes into the living room. "Yeah, then you get dese pretty babies. Ain't that right, son?" Leo walks back to his post at the door, waiting for the arrival of his brother. Teacake isn't on his mind and the question rolls off Leo as if it were never posed. "I remember Joe tellin' me when y'all started courtin' dat a light-skinned gal like yaself, wit good hair an' all, was hard to come by in these parts 'cuz ever'body is after 'em. Some of the boys still—to this day—shocked he ended up witcha."

"Let me top that off for you." Momma brings the pot of coffee over to him and pours; the cup overflows onto Teacake's leg—the good one, certain to burn.

"Oh, I'm so sorry, Teacake."

"Nah, that's awright. I understand. You probably still gettin' ovah it."

"Getting over what, Teacake?"

"Ida Mae."

"How did you know about Ida Mae?"

"Ever'body at the Nail was talkin' 'bout it. Shocked the devil outta us. But then once we thought 'bout it, we wahn't too suprised. It was jus' a matta a time, if you ask me. Jus' a matta a time."

"I should have known that people would be talkin'. Just like her to prepare ever'body for her arrival," says Momma, walking over to the screen door where Leo is. "I'm expectin' her any minute now. You know Ida Mae and Joseph don't get along too well, but it's been so long since I've seen her I'm sure he won't mind her comin' by after all these years."

" 'Comin' by?' "

"Yes. She's on her way here from Jackson. She promised she'd be here for the fireworks, so she should be sashayin' through those doors soon. Bigger than life itself."

"Anna? Anna, didn't Joe tell ya?"

Momma turns from the screen door. She can see his lips moving, but after she hears "Ida Mae's dead," nothing else seems to matter as the weight of the very house she stands in falls upon her.

Ida Mae's body had been found in an alley in the back streets of Jackson. The police said they had no clues as to how this came about. In Jackson's colored section, the story had been passed around that she had met up with some white men on the train that wanted to have their way with her. Ida Mae told them she wasn't interested, to which they replied she was just playing hard to get, so they offered her money. Ida Mae got riled and that was the last time anybody had seen her alive.

A few days after it was said to have happened, a butchershop owner found her in the alley behind his shop. Her clothes had been torn to shreds, and next to her was a green pill hat decorated with a red feather. It had ten dollars crumpled next to it, so the police ruled out the possibility of a robbery. Nobody seemed to know who the men were, but they were believed to be from up north, passing on through to Biloxi, "long gone."

Momma sits silently as Teacake tells the story as he had heard it told. Edward and Leselle have gotten up, but she doesn't even see them. Teacake says he's sorry, but he was sure that Poppa had told Momma by now. Poppa had been at the Nail when the word was going around.

"I just knowed Joe woulda tol' ya. He said he didn't know how he was gonna break the news to ya 'cuz Ida Mae was like a sista to ya and ya'd take it like losin' somebody in ya own family."

Poppa comes out of the bedroom. "Teacake, what the hell you doin' here so damn early?" Poppa looks at Momma, who stands firm, offering him nothing. No coffee. No breakfast. Not even a glance of recognition.

"I'm sorry, Joe. Hell. I thought ya tol' her. News travels fast 'round dese parts—'specially bad news. I thought ya'd told her. I swear it."

"They're here. Momma, they're here," screams Leo, running out the screen door to the yard.

"I need to wash up," says Poppa. "Teacake, I'll see you later."

"I'm sorry, Joe. Hell, ya know, I thought ya was gonna tell her. I thought she knew," Teacake says as he leaves the house, escorted by Momma's stare, though her body moves with him, too.

"Lord, give me strength," says Momma as she goes out to collect her Leon, and greet Uncle James and Auntie Clariece.

If Momma had thought Leo had not been himself, she isn't ready for what she sees in Leon. His clothes seem to fall off of him, but they can't hide the bruises on the back of his hands.

"Leon, what happened to your hands?" says Momma, taking each of them into her own. She means it as a loving, welcoming embrace, but the sight of his hands bring only shock to an awaited homecoming.

"Nothin'."

"Nothing? Then why are they all bruised?" At this point Uncle walks in. "James, what's wrong with my boy's hands? You let her do somethin' to his hands."

"You see? You see? I haven't been here one minute yet, and she's awready accusin' me of wrongdoin's," says Auntie. "That's why the boy is the way he is. No hello. No nothin'. She just starts pointin' the finger at me. Well, for your own knowledge, Missy, I never touched the boy. That's all James's doin.'"

"James, you did this?"

"Now, Anna, I know it looks worse than it actually is. You see, Leon here has been tellin' tales.

When I'd get home, thangs 'round the house would mysteriously end up broken, which never happened before he got there. When I asked him if he did it, he'd tell a story. Now, I couldn't have that. If I believe in anythang atall, I believe in the truth. I had to discipline him. A couple of swats with a ruler on the knuckles never hurt anybody. My momma used to give me much more, and I'm all the better for it. Thank you, Jesus."

"Well, James, I know, but that just doesn't sound like Leon. He's never told a fib before; why would he want to start now?" says Momma, waiting for an answer, though none can prove reasonable.

Poppa has been standing in the room for some time, his hands behind his back, as if he too might receive a few unwarranted swats.

This was how our family reunion began. Leon went in the room with his brothers. Uncle James soon went back to the car. He was always on the go, leaving us to handle Auntie.

Momma was still not over the news about Ida Mae. She hadn't had time to digest it, and now she had this, too, to contend with. When Leon spoke, it was just above a whisper, and he seemed to have picked up a stutter. Auntie would ask him something and he'd mumble something back. She'd tell him to speak up. Poppa just sat there, trying to stay out of the way.

The day went by, my kicking every step of the

way. Momma tried to keep from causing trouble, but Auntie was truly trying on the nerves.

The boys had been playing in their room for most of the day. Leon started to get the color back into his skin and he looked like he was at home. Momma was fixing supper in the kitchen, an earshot away from Auntie and Poppa in the living room. Again, he had dressed for the occasion.

"Still no job, Li'l Man? I s'pose this is what you do all day. Just sit in this here livin' room and let your chilren run 'round doin' whatever they please. Maybe I oughta just take the whole lot of 'em next time. It'd do 'em good to see how thangs s'posed to be."

Junior walked in. His face didn't change. It was as if he'd been preparing all day for seeing Auntie and in that, no pleasantries were possible, not even for appearances' sake. He stood there refusing to mirror Auntie's smile.

"Well, here is the man of the house. Come on in here and give me a hug. Boy, you lookin' more and more like Ma Dear ever'day. Ain't he, Li'l Man?"

"Yessum," said Poppa.

"How you doin', Auntie Clariece?" was the most Junior could bring himself to utter.

"Fine. I'm just fine, praise the Lawd. Though my arthritis tends to act up ever' now and again. You see, a preacher's wife is always on the go. No rest for the weary."

"We all have our crosses to bear. I'm sure it's not all that bad. Where's Leon?"

"He's in there with the rest of them. Keepin' up all that racket! Quiet down up in there!"

"*You* don't need to tell him that; he's at home now."

"Well, yes, Junior, I s'pose he is. Li'l Man, why don't you sit up straight? You always slumpin' down. I guess that's just your way. You was always slumpin' over, even when you walk.

"You wanna hear somethin' funny, Li'l Man? That son of yourn tried runnin' away when we got him home. I guess the boy didn't realize that we live some thirty miles from here 'cuz I woke up one mornin' and he had up and gone. Got quite a ways, too. James went after him in our car. Y'all really should think about gettin' yaself a car. 'Course, I s'pose Junior here would have to get it, now wouldn't he?

"As I was sayin', James picked him up a good bit down the road and gave him a hidin' not soon to be forgotten. Just like Ma Dear gave you when she went after you that time you ran off. 'Course, myself, I never touches the boy. That James's job. I try and stop him when I think he's gone too far, bein' of a womanly nature and all. But the good Reverend knows best, so naturally, I let him do what he thinks best."

"Yes, I'm sure you do," said Junior, then started walking toward the bedroom.

"Junior, could you send Leon out here? I want him to tell Li'l Man how he tried to run away," said

Auntie. A few seconds, later Leon came out of the room, with the other boys in tow. Momma, too, came to the kitchen door to oversee the telling of this story.

"Leon, tell your poppa how you tried to run away." Leon stood there without a word. In the short time he'd been back, Momma had noticed that he would now put his hand up around his mouth whenever he was spoken to. This was new to her. "Leon, now stand up straight and take ya hand away from yo' mouth. What I tell you 'bout that? You hear me speakin' to you? Now open your mouth and speak up."

"Supper's ready," said Momma.

"Now, don't you shame me, Leon. I said, tell your Poppa how you tried to run away and your Uncle James had to—"

"And I said, supper is ready."

The tone in Momma's voice hushed the room. The world outside continued to move. The wind rustling in the cornfields, the popping from the chain on the porch swing swaying—all these things went on as usual, but in the living room, everything stayed trapped in time, except desperate eyes trying to find a spot to rest as they glanced from corner to corner, attempting to focus on anything other than anyone else. Only Momma's eyes remained still, centered directly on Auntie.

"Okay, fine. Fine, Anna," says Auntie with a tension-breaking laugh. "Don't break your water."

"Come on, Leon. I made your favorite: chicken and dumplings," says Momma, picking up where the silence left off. Leon dropped his hand from his mouth and went over to Momma. She put her arms around him. All of her attention was on him, and he needed it so. "The dumplings are real thick, just like you like them."

Auntie Clariece went into the kitchen as well, taking her place at the head of the table.

"Junior, I saw you with a Bible earlier, somethin' Li'l Man pro'bly hasn't picked up since he was a boy. Why don't you come sit here and bless the meal that your lovely Momma was so dear to fix." Auntie got up from her seat—Poppa's seat—but Junior just looked at Poppa. "Make ace now, the food's gettin' cold." Still Junior didn't move. "Li'l Man, tell him to come on and lead us in a prayer. What is wrong up in this house? Don't nobody mind they elders when they say somethin'?"

Poppa could have been Leon had your eyes been closed, for when he did finally tell Junior to do what his Auntie said, it measured nothing more than a mumble. Junior got up and went to the head of the table and I kicked like never before. Momma never winced. She looked at every face at that table, ending with Junior's as the prayer dribbled from his mouth: "Jesus wept."

After supper, Auntie told Poppa to come out on the porch so they could "catch up." Momma always feared these private sittings; they always seemed to mean trouble. Momma told the twins to go into the bedroom. She was hoping if they had some time to themselves, Leon would get back to his old self.

Junior, Edward, and Leselle helped clear the table. Momma stood over the dishwater and the steam rose, moistening her face. But with me as big as I was and moving around so, she had to step away from the sink.

"You awright, Momma?" Junior walked Momma to a chair. Edward and Leselle picked up the rest of the dishes.

"Yes, Junior, as fine as I can be. Just a dizzy spell, that's all. Your li'l sister is stayin' busy. And it's been a long day."

"Sorry 'bout Ida Mae."

Hearing this came as a shock—even Junior knew. But she was too tired to worry herself about that. Though her body ached, as if second nature, her voice took over. "Me, too. Me, too. I kept waitin' for her to walk in that door at any minute with that canarylike grin on her face, makin' ever'thing all right. She had a way, that one did, just a way about her that you knew she'd say the right thing, make it all better. That gal could turn bitter lemons to sweet lemonade. But not this time. No, not this time."

"*Ow!*" Momma turned around. Edward was waving his hand through the air like it was on fire.

"What's wrong, Edward?"

"I was gonna wash up these supper dishes."

"Come here, and let me see your hand. It's not too bad. Leselle, bring me some butter."

Momma took the butter and rubbed it in her hand
and then onto Edward's skin like she always did
with the olive oil on her own skin each morning.

"I do appreciate your wantin' to help, as does
your li'l sister. But that water is too hot for you to
go stickin' your hand in that sink. Didn't you see
the steam comin' up off of it?"

"Yes'm. But your hands was in it, and it didn't
burn you."

"Yes, they were, but the hands of mommas don't
burn so easily. They get used to the temperature.
After a while, it doesn't hurt anymore."

Unfortunately, the butter loved the heat of his
hand—an old wives' tale gone bad. It didn't matter,
though, for it was the touch that took the pain away.
She kept rubbing his hands as she spoke, and when
she was finished, she asked him if a kiss would make
it all feel better. Edward said that that was all right,
now that he was twelve "and a half," he was getting
too old for his momma to be kissing him. Momma
said she supposed he was right, but she'd give him
one just this one last time. And she did.

When the boys went to their room to get ready
for bed, Auntie Clariece came in from the porch,
Poppa trailing behind her. Momma braced herself
for whatever news was coming, but nothing un-
usual presented itself, just the woman that would
be my momma, being her usual self.

"You 'bout ready to drop that baby, Anna?" said
Auntie. "Ever'body in the congregation is waitin'

for my li'l boy to grace our church. The Reverend always mentions it at service, that it 'won't be long now.' And the peoples are so nice. They had an extra collection offerin' just for the baby. Ever'body gave somethin' and nobody took out change. You ain't goin' to have to worry 'bout this baby needin' a thang. 'Course, by no means is we goin' to spoil him. Ain't no such thing as no spoilt colored chile. At least not a *real* colored chile. But I s'pose that ain't your fault, now is it? But don'tcha worry your never mind. Since them twins came out lookin' like they do, it's 'bout time for our blood to kick in again.

"I've already picked out a nice li'l church ensemble for him. Yes, it's goin' to be right fine, him sittin' on my lap on the first pew, up close where he can see his poppa, the Reverend James Caldwell.

"When we first told the congregation, you shoulda seen the women in the church. They knew that a baby meant the Reverend was mine for good. You shoulda just seen the green in they eyes. And you know colored folks ain't got no green eyes— least not *real* colored folks.

"Yeah, most of the women on the Auxiliary Board walked 'round like younguns in heat. Just as fast as they wanna be. Speakin' of, whatever happened to that ol' gal who stood up by you at you and Li'l Man's weddin'? The moment I saw her walk in the house of the Lawd, I knew she had no bizness in nobody's white dress. Somebody told me she moved up north and was doin' all sorts of devilment."

Poppa raised his head for the first time and looked at Momma. I kicked real hard—the hardest yet—and Momma moaned, but if it was due to me, I can't rightly say.

"Her name was Ida Mae, and she has passed on, so I don't reckon that 'the Lawd' cares one way or another what she's wearin' or doin', so why should you?" Momma took a deep breath, then looked at Poppa, then back at Auntie. "If you'll excuse me, I've been on my feet all day, workin', and I'm goin' to fix myself a pallet in the livin' room so I can get some rest. I've turned back our bed for you. I hope you have a good night's sleep."

"My, my, my," said Auntie as Momma walked out of the kitchen.

Momma went in to check on the boys. Everybody always seemed to go to bed earlier when Auntie was visiting. It was just easier. At their door, she listened for a moment and heard movement, so she knocked. Junior's voice said, "Come in."

"Ever'body all right in here? Edward, how's that hand?" said Momma.

"Awright."

"Let me have a look-see."

"I said it's awright!"

Junior jumped up from his bed. "Boy, don't you talk to Momma like that or I'll—"

"Junior! Junior, sit down."

Junior did as Momma said, and though Edward was too old to be kissed, he wasn't too old to start crying, and on down the line it flowed—Leselle, Leon, Leo. Junior got up and stormed out the room, leaving the door open. With all of them crying and Junior walking out, Momma didn't know who or what to try to fix first.

"I'm sorry. I'm sorry," said Momma, and she started to leave. As she reached their door, Auntie screamed out, "Leon? Leon, come on in here and give me some good-night sugar."

"He's asleep, Clariece. Let him be. Please, just let him be."

... You're gone and I write to you as if you still might walk through those doors. They say the spirit lives forever, but they only say it after someone is already gone. It seems too late at that point. It makes no sense. So much doesn't.

Clariece is here. She treats J. T. like a child and there's nothing I can do. Some things have to be done for oneself. I know that's easy to say when—

"What you writin'?"

"Clariece? I thought you were in bed."

"Just thought I'd have drink of water."

"Let me get it for you."

"No, don't get up. I can get it. Look here, Anna. I know we've had our differences, but I'm sorry about your friend. I know how close you were to her. Pity."

"Thank you, Clariece. That's very nice of you."

"Well, you're not to blame for it. Livin' that kind of life, she dug her grave; now she can be buried in it. You have a good night's rest now."

I was cut off, once again. The Reverend must truly be the holiest man alive. I was taught to find the good in people, but if there is any within her, it's definitely hiding. Maybe a baby is just what she needs . . .

"Junior? Junior, ever'body is asleep," says Momma, walking out on the back porch, seeing her child now in a man's form. "You been out here a long time; you must be gettin' tired yourself. It's a nice night, though. Peaceful. I can go and get you some quilts and make you a nice pallet out here if you like. The mosquitoes haven't been too bad this year, which is surprisin' with all the rain we've been gettin'. Usually by this time of year, ever'body is walkin' around itchin' and scratchin' like dogs.

"Yeah. Well, I guess you don't want to talk. That's fine. I just want you to know that . . . know that you're not alone. I understand. It's been hard on you, I know. Nobody knows like me. You've had to take on quite a few hardships and had to be around when you'd probably rather have been with people your own age, doin' things that people your age do. Believe it or not, I was your age once, so I know.

"You've grown up to be a right fine man, Junior. That's what you are now. You're a man, just like your Poppa. Oh, yes you are. Don't you sit there shruggin' and rollin' your eyes at me. You're just like him. The hardest thing in the world to do is look at yourself.

"You got so much to express, to say. But you don't ever do it. You just let it build up and build up, till it can't anymore. Then somebody else who—doesn't even understand why—gets it all. That's how things keep on goin', how limbs from family trees get broken. People are too busy transplantin' their trunks from yard to yard with the same ol' stuff in them, things they should have just left behind with the change of the seasons. The cycle keeps going. You understand?

"Look at me. I said, look at me. Ever'body in this big world isn't goin' to be like me, like Momma. At least not like this momma. You see, I can come to you. I can ask you what's the matter and let you take it out on me, because I love you. And I'd rather you deal with what you need to deal with with me than let it build up inside of you, boilin' till it overflows. Junior, mommas see it all. We understand the explosions, but we still try and stop them from happenin'. That's what we do. I know you're angry. You . . . you have ever' right to be.

"Well. You don't have to talk now if you don't

want to. That's fine. But that's exactly what I'm talkin' about. You can't just let it all sit there. It'll eat you up inside. Steal your heart, your soul. And once a man loses those things, all he can do is wait to be buried, because more than likely, he already feels dead.

"What I'm tryin' to say to you, Junior, is you can't ever kill somethin' that doesn't even believe it's alive. But understandin', understandin' can lead to changin' that. Understand?

"I know you *hear* what I'm sayin', but I hope you're *listenin'*. You are a good son—have been for some seventeen years. Lord, seventeen years. I guess that means I'm gettin' on up there, too, doesn't it? But you are a good son. Never a bit of trouble. Had a smile that could light up the night. Too bad I haven't seen it lately.

"And you've been a good brother, too. And your brothers need you now, more than ever. I know you can sit out here on this back porch and look out yonder at a world that's yours for the takin', wonderin' why things are this way or that way. But you are a man now. To wonder why is to live in the past. You're too good for that, Junior. You've got too many people that love you, depend on you. You hear me?

"I'm sorry about the way things are, and I'll do ever'thin' in my power to make them better. But you have to stop blamin' and start livin'. I can only

say I'm sorry so many times, because then it starts
to not mean anythin'.

"We need you, your brothers and me, and your
poppa, too. Yes, he does! I know that's hard to believe, but it's true. He needs you, Junior. Not to
mention this little bundle of joy. She's going to be
so proud that you're her big brother."

"Too bad she ain't gonna be 'round to ever
know," says Junior, opening his mouth for the first
time, getting up from the back-porch steps. "Stay
out here if you want to, but I'm goin' to bed. I gotta
be at the mill early tomorrow."

Momma sits stiller than a held breath, a heart
not beating.

Momma was the first up, closely followed by
Auntie Clariece, who in turn woke up Poppa. She
told him it was "bad manners" for him to sleep
later than his guest. Momma said that she wasn't a
guest at all. Auntie looked at her, then Momma
added, "I mean, you're family, Clariece." Even still,
whatever the meaning behind Momma's words,
Auntie Clariece wanted Poppa up.

"Li'l Man, I think it'd be more than nice if we go
pay Ma Dear a visit at the graveyard today. I know
you pro'bly haven't been there since she died,
which any decent person oughta be 'shamed of. It
ain't but a hop, skip, and a jump from here. It'll be
nice for us to go together. We can pick some flowers
from the yard to take with us. I'm sure Anna won't

mind me takin' some of 'em. Will you, Anna? 'Course you don't," said Auntie, not waiting for Momma's reply. Poppa didn't say a thing. He just went in and started to get dressed.

"And stand up straight, Li'l Man. You goin' to get a hump in your back if you don't watch out."

Junior came out of the room next. He looked at Momma; Momma looked at him. He smiled. Momma, relieved by the sight, smiled back, releasing the bear on her back, livening her step.

"Junior, why don't you join your ol' auntie for some breakfast."

"Sorry, Auntie, I gotta get to work early today. The Fourth's got us backed up at the plant."

"I tell you, I don't ever get to spend no time witchu. You're always on the go. Go, go, go! I guess that's your age showin'."

"I guess it is. We all gotta show our age at some time," said Junior as he looked at Momma. "Momma, I'll be home 'fore dark. We gettin' off early for the holiday. If I get back in time, I'll take the boys to get some firecrackers for tomorrow."

"That'll be nice, Junior," said Momma. "I'm sure your brothers would like that very much."

Junior and Momma smiled at each other again, and Junior said 'bye to Auntie Clariece as he walked out of the kitchen to begin his day.

"He has just grown up to be a fine young man," said Auntie. "Just so handsome. Looks just like Ma Dear."

"Yes. Yes, he has, Clariece. All my boys are fine."

"Well, just know that I'll be a good mother to this baby. James and I have already picked a name."

Momma grabbed the dishrag and held tight.

"It was easy, really. We decided it would be best if we just named the baby after James. James Junior."

Poppa walked in.

"Li'l Man, I was just tellin' Anna here that we've decided to name the baby after James. Don't you think that's nice?"

"Anythang you say, Clariece."

The boys came in the kitchen. Good-mornings were exchanged, not to anyone in particular, just in general. That didn't seem to sit right with Auntie. She made Leon give her "good-mornin' sugar" and had him sit by her till she was finished with her breakfast. Momma couldn't sit for very long. Between fixing everybody's plate, my kicking, and her excusing herself to the bathroom, she was forever on the move.

After breakfast, or at least the eating of it, the cleaning was left for Momma to do. Auntie made Poppa get changed for the graveyard, for what he had on wasn't presentable, "not even for the dead," and though she was used to being driven around, she wouldn't mind walking to pay tribute to her "dear Ma Dear."

Momma talked Auntie out of taking Leon, but all the boys stayed in their room until she had gone.

Auntie walked out the door with Poppa at her heels, but before continuing on, she stopped and cut some petunias to place on the grave.

"Anna," screamed Auntie from the yard, "the weeds seem to be takin' over out here. You oughta do somethin' 'bout that."

Momma walked over to the screen door, watching Auntie with the flowers. And just as if talking to the screen, she said, "Yes. For once Clariece, I think you're right."

... Even without you here, the fireworks go on. But I'm not afraid of them anymore ...

"Ida Mae? Ida Mae, where are you?" said Anna, walking along the creek. It was the Fourth of July, many moons before. Anna had been put on "restriction," and Missus Anderson wouldn't let her go to the fireworks. "Ida Mae, this isn't funny, now. If you're out here, then come on out. I mean it. Ida Mae? I'm not scared. And if anybody else is out here, I just want you to know I'm not scared. And I know you're there. So . . . so, if you're watching me—"

"Boo," screamed Ida Mae. Anna screamed as well.

"I thought you weren't scared. 'I'm not scared. And if anybody else . . .' "

"Okay, Ida Mae. You got me," said Anna with

her hand still on her heart. "Sorry I was late, but Momma was restless tonight and I had to really scheme to get out of the house."

"That's awright. Hell, the night's still young. I'll pro'bly go 'round the Nail. But I bought us some-thin' first."

"Ida Mae, I don't want a drink."

"Now there you go. Why is it that ever' time I say I bought us somethin', you gotta go and think it's somethin' to drink. That hurts my feelin's, Anna. It really does," said Ida Mae. Her speech was followed by an uncomfortable moment, then Ida Mae started laughing. Anna, relieved, started to laugh, too, as Ida Mae pulled out a bottle of Scotch, "the latest drink up north."

"But you don't mind if I have a li'l, do you?"

"Suit yourself. Ida Mae? You think things'll change between you and me when I marry Joseph?"

"Change? When y'all get married?"

"Yes. You think they will? Between you and me?"

"Girl, he hasn't even asked you yet."

"But I know he's going to, sooner or later."

"You see, that's your problem. You go on and on 'bout somethin' that you don't even know is gonna happen. You talkin' about the weddin' when there ain't even a groom yet. You see, that's how you get hurt."

"That's not true. I don't do that. Not any more

than you talk about going 'up north,' " said Anna, standing up and looking down at Ida Mae. "If I had a nickel for ever' time you said 'up north' this and 'up north' that, I'd be a rich woman. So don't try and tell me that I'm not allowed to think about me and Joseph gettin' married."

"You're right, precious. I'm sorry."

"Well, I'm sorry, too, Ida Mae. I'm sorry that ever'body else can dream and do things, and other people let them do it, but whenever I open my mouth to say somethin', nobody listens or takes me seriously. Seems to me ever'body is allowed to dream about things but me."

Anna stood looking over the creek. The moon shimmied brightly across the water's top, but it only darkened what existed below.

"Maybe that's 'cuz most of the people 'round here been here all they lives and gonna be here till they die. All they have is their talk to keep them thinkin' they movin' on even though they standin' still," said Ida Mae, standing and walking toward the water as if talking to the fish confined to the creek, the creek in which she and Anna had learned to swim.

"You see, Anna, you think people don't care about what you say. But hear me when I say they do. I know. They hear you when you say anythang. If they 'fess up to it or not, they hear you. But they

don't want to, you see. They don't want to, 'cuz
when they hear you sayin' somethin' that you think
is just a dream, they know that for you, it will
pro'bly come true.

"They look at you and, for many of them, they
wish they was you. Why you think they all used to
pick at you, call you names? That's 'cuz they was
jealous. They wanted to be like you. You was livin'
their dreams. Your family has money, you live in
that big house with Missus Anderson, and ever'-
body looks up to her. They all would have switched
places with you in a minute."

"That's not true . . ."

"Oh, Anna, grow up! Grow up, damn you. You
say you want people to listen to what you say? Then
start sayin' somethin' 'sides what you think you
s'posed to say. Until then, I don't really want to
hear how nobody listens to you. 'Cuz till you mean
what you say and say what you mean, you can't
even listen to yaself."

Again, there was a moment of thick silence.

"I'm sorry, precious," said Ida Mae. "You pro'bly
will marry Joseph. You can have anythang you
want. Truth be told, I'm kinda jealous of you, too.
Don't look so suprised. I am. And you know, the
thing that hurts me the most is, I can't even be mad
when you get what you want, 'cuz I know you. And
'cuz I do, I know you deserve the best."

Anna and Ida Mae hugged and Ida Mae started to cry. That was the first time Anna had ever seen Ida Mae cry. She had once told Anna she had no more tears, that they were all used up.

"See there. You got all 'motional on me, makin' me forget about my present," said Ida Mae, wiping the tears from her eyes and walking to her bag. First, she pulled out an empty bottle.

"Ida Mae, I told you I didn't want a drink."

"That's good, 'cuz you not gonna get one. But you need an empty bottle if you want to shoot a bottle rocket."

Ida Mae pulled out two bottle rockets, one for each of them. She brought the bottle rockets because last Fourth, Anna had popped a firecracker in her hand. Now she only shoots bottle rockets so that when she lights them, she still has time to run for cover before the explosion. The memory of the accident the previous year was probably the reason Missus Anderson had so conveniently put her on restriction that year.

They walked to the edge of the creek. Ida Mae put the bottles down and they placed their bottle rockets in them, angling them so each would light up the night in different directions.

"Wait. You didn't answer my question," said Anna as Ida Mae was bending down to light the stem.

"What question?"

"Do you think things will change between us when I get married?"

"I'm sure in some ways it will. Ever'thang else does."

"That's not what I wanted to hear."

"I know."

Ida Mae handed Anna a match. They both struck their matches, and on the count of three, they bent down to light their bottle rockets together.

They ran as fast as they could to get away from the fizzing in order to get a good look at those rockets shooting toward a sky full of possibilities.

The spark of each stem reached the gunpowder at the same time. The rockets, with a noise that sounded like someone shushing someone in church, headed toward the deep blue night, leaving a trail of gray smoke.

When the rockets reached their peak, Ida Mae's let off an aggressive sound that ended its exciting journey. Though Anna's reached into the night, too, they waited and listened for the sound it never made.

9

The lingering smell of oatmeal fills the house this afternoon. These last few hours have been the first in some time that Momma's had her children to herself. She had made the batter in her biggest bowl.

Leselle was the first to discover Momma was making cookies, and it hadn't taken long for him to spread the word, making all the boys appear, one after the other, by Momma's side at the kitchen table. Faces filled with anticipation, they watch Momma mix the batter, adding butter she had taken out hours earlier to soften, then cinnamon and raisins. Their eyes are open wide, and even I can hear their swallows.

The big wooden bowl rests between Momma's arm and her diaphragm, muscles tightening in each as she stirs. I, too, stir, and with each movement, nearer to her hips I fall. Throughout the day, Momma had continued to say, "At any moment. At any moment."

The boys say very little. They watch Momma like she's doing a magic trick. Momma lays the cookies in little globs on the waxed paper. The oven has been turned on and the heat of the kitchen says it's ready to do its part. When all the batter has been placed in neat rows, just far enough apart as not to touch one another once they begin taking shape, Momma slides the cookies into the oven.

"Well, it won't be long now," Momma says, teasingly. She knows this routine too well. The boys can't care less about the cookies that are thirty minutes away. They're concerned with the here and now. What they're really standing in this kitchen waiting for is the rights to the big wooden spoon and bowl that have batter stuck to them.

"Now, if you boys want to go on outside and play, I'll give you a holler when the cookies are done. I'm just going to wash up this bowl and spoon . . ."

"Momma?"

"Yes, Leon?"

"If you—I mean, we could wash that up for you. If you want."

Though I can feel myself being jiggled around, Momma keeps a straight face. She plays along with her sons as if it were the first time.

"Yeah, and we'll keep an eye out on the cookies while they're bakin'," adds Leselle.

"Yeah, Momma, and you could sit down and rest for a while. We know you're probably real tired," says Leo.

"It's so hot in here, you might get dizzy. So we'll just handle the washin' up," says Edward.

"So you'll wash this bowl and spoon for me? And watch the cookies?"

"Yes'm," say the four together like the church's junior choir.

"Well then, I guess I wouldn't mind goin' out for some fresh air. But if you need any help in here, just give me a shout. I'll be out front."

"No, we won't need nothin', Momma. Just you go rest," says Edward.

"Now, Edward, you sure that hand is better? I wouldn't want you to burn yourself again, sticking your hand in the hot dishwater."

"Oh, no, ma'am. It's all better. See? Good as new. It was the kiss, I guess. 'Sides, I'll check it with my finger 'fore I stick my whole hand in it."

"Okay, then. You be sure you do that, or I might have to kiss it again."

Momma walks out of the kitchen with a grin wide enough to wrap the kitchen that holds her sons. She stands just outside the door and hears her children, my brothers, going to work, but no washing is involved. When they're finished, she knows that that bowl and spoon will be licked clean, but she will still have to wash them; by then, the cookies will be done, and the bowl and spoon will soon be forgotten, until the next time.

. . . Who do I write to now? I've not had a moment to cry. I'm holding on now because if I don't, I'm sure to fall.

At one time, they were letters to you. Now, they are you. Help, now lost . . .

The sky is clear today. The boys are out and about just running around. Since Leon's return, they all seem closer. There have been no fights, just laughter. Momma said it sometimes takes a person being separated from another before they can truly appreciate what it is they have.

Momma's taking deep breaths and the air is fresh. We're in the front yard while she's weeding the garden. Though she'd normally use a hoe, today she's doing it by hand. She watches her boys running around the yard, and their screams dance in her ears. She smiles. I kick.

Leon comes and sits by our side. "You need some help, Momma?"

"No, thank you, Leon. I don't want to stop you from your fun." Leon gets up and starts to walk away. Every few steps he looks back at Momma. He stops for a moment, then comes back to our side. "Momma, do you and Poppa still love me?"

The question slaps Momma. And when she remembers she can speak, she says, "Yes, Leon. More each day." Leon smiles for the first time since he's been back.

"You sure you don't need any help?" says Leon.

"You know what you can do? Why don't you go check the mail. That would be a big help."

Leon runs off. When he returns, the envelope he carries has Momma's name on it. With this chore done, he joins our brothers at play, never knowing he has slapped Momma twice while trying to be helpful.

Momma knows the handwriting like she knows her own. She looks at the envelope for a long time, then runs her fingers along its edges, stopping near the seal. A letter used to serve as a sign of how close Ida Mae was and that she would soon be here. Now, it's a reminder that she isn't coming.

Momma, as gently as if rubbing me, even after I've kicked, breaks the seal, pulls out the piece of paper, and unfolds it, then again, and then again until the page, full of words, stares at her. She looks in the distance. Seeing no one, she begins to read:

Dearest Precious,

I'm on my way to Jackson. I'm missin' Chicago awready, but I can't wait to see your smilin' face, not to mention those twins I haven't set eyes on yet. I hope they ain't growin' up to be like they stanky poppa (smile).

I've got all kinds of kinks from bein' on this

train. Not for the company of some soldiers from up north heading down to Biloxi, I wouldn't be having any fun. Those white boys love to flirt. They think just 'cuz they white, they can have their way witcha. I must say, the only thang better than a man in a uniform is a man from the north in uniform. 'Course, I only look now. My sax man sees to that. But just 'cuz you tryin' to lose weight don't mean you can't look at the menu (smile).

Now, you tell that Joseph that I'm gonna be comin' by the house and I don't means for no trouble from him. You know I just poke fun at him 'cuz I love you. I'll make peace wit him when I get there. I promise. He a good man. If that sista of his didn't raise him after his momma died, he probably would have been okay. Speaking of, is she dead yet? If she is, I know she went to heaven 'cuz even the devil wouldn't let her in hell (smile).

I still plan to come before the fireworks, hopefully on the third. It all just 'pends on if or not I run into anythang intrastin' in that place they calls a city. But Jackson has always been good to me.

I can't wait to see you. I know you pretty as all get out, 'cuz remember, like I always say, "Black don't crack" (smile).

I'm gonna stop here. The porter is coming

through and I wants to give it to him to mail off
at the next stop. He kinda cute, too (smile).
All my love,
Ida Mae

Momma folds the letter, then again, then again,
and puts it back in the envelope. She looks up the
walk, but there's nobody there. She looks at the pile
of weeds that she's pulled out and begins pulling
out more, certain others are waiting to take their
place. Homeless crickets begin rubbing their legs
together as the day's sun edges its way down.

Momma is quiet for a long time. She just keeps
pulling up the weeds, trying her best to get to the
roots. A crash coming from the kitchen stops her,
and we slowly get up and, as best we can, run into
the house. There is a shattered Mason jar on the
floor. The boys are standing over it, looking at
Momma, no one claiming the broken pieces.

"What happened?"

"I didn't do it, I promise. I didn't do it," says
Leon. He's almost in tears. He's standing in the corner of the living room with his hands behind his
back, looking at the broken jar, repeating that he
hadn't done it.

"Come here, Leon."

"But I didn't do it. I promise," he says, his crying
getting heavier with each step closer to Momma.

"It's fine, precious. It's fine. It's just a jar. It's
fine."

Momma reaches out her arms to hug him and Leon flinches, his body stiffening. Momma takes him in her arms and I can feel my brother pressed against me. With his face on Momma's stomach, he says, "Please don't send me back. I'll be good. I promise."

"I know you will. I know you will, precious."

All the other boys came toward us. Momma tells them to watch where they walk, not wanting the glass to wound.

What Leon has to say after he calms down makes Momma react in a way I have never—in my almost nine months—seen. Leon tells stories of how Auntie would break things, then when Uncle James came home, she'd place the blame on him, for which Uncle James would give him a beating to discipline him.

On Leon's first day there, Auntie gave him some money. And then when Uncle came home that night, she claimed that a silver dollar was missing from her drawer and that nobody else had been around. When Uncle called Leon from his room and made him empty his pockets, there was her silver dollar, sinfully shiny.

Leon didn't understand what the beatings were for half of the time. Auntie had convinced him that there would be no reason for him to try calling her a liar, because Uncle James would never take his word over hers. And how right she was.

There would be days when Uncle was away

preaching, and when he returned, Auntie would have come up with some story about something Leon had done wrong. It was as if she spent her days conjuring up things, because as the "preacher's wife," that was really the only way to fill her hollow days. She was clever enough not to overdo it, but for Leon, it seemed like a daily occurrence.

He said Uncle was nice to him, and so was Auntie when Uncle was present, which wasn't often enough, leaving Leon to fill the void.

Uncle would always bring him back presents from his trips. But whenever Auntie saw this, she would always come up with some tale about Leon, saying that he didn't deserve a present and that it should be given to the children's center at the church. "No gifts for the guilty," she would tell Uncle James. And of course, Uncle, trusting Auntie's judgment, would do as she said. Auntie never laid a hand on Leon, but to hurt him, she never had to. That was her way.

As Leon tells the story, Momma holds him tighter, as each sentence only seems to get worse, sucking the breath from both of us. The pain the stories hold is small compared to the guilt that shades her heart, the heart that keeps me alive.

Momma releases Leon. She raises her head high and her voice resonated: "I'm not giving that woman my baby."

A smile comes across Leon's face. I'm certain he thinks she's talking about him. In some way, I'm sure she is. But I can feel that she's talking about me—Lisa.

... This new child is coming soon. Clariece keeps calling it him. There's so much she doesn't know.

Even a child can teach, if we choose to listen. We have to want to hear, because the voice may be nothing more than a whisper, if that.

My boys have been running around like true brothers. There haven't been any fights. I try and guess what they talk about when they're in their room. If children don't know everything about their parents, I guess it's safe to say we don't know everything about them.

This baby may be a girl, but she kicks like a boy—hard and often.

This will have to be my last letter to you. I can't write anymore. I'm wearing the lipstick you gave me. I can feel your spirit. That will have to be enough. Thank you.

Love, now and forever,

Anna

The *Free Press* had found its way to our front porch. The colored paper was always called the "picture paper" because there were always more pictures than words. There's a need to see colored faces in print, to show we exist. But that story was one that was certain to be read by all.

There was no more walking on the edge. At long last, the fall had been witnessed. Ida Mae's death led to many hours of over-the-fence conversation, until the next piece of gossip stole the memory of the big letters on the top of the page: LOCAL GIRL FOUND DEAD IN JACKSON.

An old picture of Ida Mae topped the front page, a shot from the Rusty Nail. She was smiling. Momma cut out the picture, and holding it, she said, "Was it all you thought it would be?"

Momma sees Auntie and Poppa coming up the road. We've been on the porch, waiting. She walks to the screen door and yells for the boys to hurry.

Auntie and Poppa start through the gate and up the walk toward the porch. Momma watches them, never saying a word.

"My goodness! I tell you, Anna, I have worked up such an appetite from walkin', I can pro'bly even enjoy some of your cookin'," says Auntie, walking up the steps and onto the porch. "I guess my feet just aren't used to this kind of treatment. 'Course, havin' a car can just spoil you rotten."

Auntie goes into the house, followed by Poppa, then Momma.

"Smells like cookies up in here. That'll be a nice dessert. I hope you didn't give any to Leon before supper. It'll ruin his appetite. He's awready in need of some meat on his bones. I tried to fatten him up while he was with us, but he just wouldn't eat. Sickly li'l ol' thang, ain't he?"

Auntie walks into the kitchen. Momma stands in the living room.

"Supper's not ready?" says Auntie.

"Boys! Boys, are you ready?"

The boys appear at their bedroom door. They look like a family picture standing in the frame of that door. Auntie comes out of the kitchen, asking why the food isn't ready, and she sees the suitcase.

"What's going on here?"

"That's a good question, Clariece. Because you see, 'here' is just the problem," says Momma. "We're leaving."

"Leavin'? Chile, don't be silly. You too close to passin' that baby, so this ain't no time for you to think you gonna be runnin' ever' whicha way, *scalavantin'* 'round. I tell you, Li'l Man, older this gal gets, the crazier she gets. Come out here and talk some sense into her."

Momma walks over to the boys and leads them toward the screen door. She tells them to wait there. She then walks past Auntie and goes into the kitchen. She's very calm. She doesn't want to make a scene in front of the boys.

"Me and *my* chilren, all of my chilren, are leavin'," says Momma, so softlike that it almost sounds like she's telling the biggest of secrets. She has no trouble finding the right words and no trouble saying them, though the taste they leave in her mouth makes her sick. Poppa raises his head as if the rooster had lost track of time and crowed out of turn.

"What?"

"What I said was, me and my chilren are leavin' this house. Now, the two of us can sit here quietly and try to handle this in a civilized way, or you can have it another way. But either way, I'm leavin' and I'm takin' the boys and this baby with me."

"Li'l Man, I can't believe you're goin' to sit here while this . . . this woman is talkin' 'bout takin' my baby from me."

Momma walks real close to Auntie, so close that their breaths bounce off each other's face.

"You know, Clariece, your name should be Manerva, because you've been on my nerves for years. *Your* baby? Do you truly believe after what you've done to Leon that you've got a baby comin'? If you do, then you're a bit confused about who's gettin' crazier ever'day. But if you'd like to see just how crazy I can be, be my guest, Clariece. Just be warned, pregnant or not, I go for the head first. Ida Mae taught me that."

"Anna, I don't have any idea of what you're talkin' 'bout."

"No. You wouldn't, would you?"

"What did that li'l lyin' mouth say? Leon, come in here!"

Auntie walks out to the living room, where the

boys are still standing by the door. She reaches
for Leon.

"If you touch him, you'd better make sure you
mean it," said Momma. Auntie stops and turns
toward Momma.

"I told you he's been tellin' tales. Wait till the
Reverend hears about this, Leon; just you wait."

"Well, you'll have to wait till hell freezes over,
because you nor the Reverend will ever touch any
of these chilren again. What you do to J. T., that's
one thing. That's between you and him. He's a
grown man now. He's responsible for that. But you
will not treat these chilren that way."

Momma looks Auntie Clariece square in the
rounds of her eyes. There's no elephant on the end
table for good luck, no dishrag to hold, no Gram or
Ida Mae to back her up. This time, she has to stand
on her own.

She turns to Poppa, who's still sitting at the
kitchen table.

"Joseph, I love you. I do. Sometimes I have to ask
myself why, but the only answer is 'because.' But
'because' is not an answer . . . not enough of an
answer anymore. I'll be at my momma's house."

"Li'l Man! Li'l Man, you goin' to sit there? You
just goin' to sit there in your house while this . . .
this gal talks to you like she the man of the house?
Boy, your boys are standin' at the door in your
house and ready to go . . ."

"I'm not givin' this woman my child to raise.

She's not fit to be a mother." Momma never raises her voice, never seems angry. The time for anger has long since passed. Now is the time to begin again. "J. T., I know it was my fault to let you offer my baby over without sayin' anythin'. I know it was my fault when you sent Leon to her behind my back and I didn't do anythin'. Well, I'm sick to my stomach of things bein' my fault. But I'll tell you one thing, Clariece. My momma raised a lady, but if you ever, ever touch as much as one hair on any of my chilren, I swear to you, it will take 'the Lawd' that you so like to call on to get me off of you. Do you understand me? Because I want to make it clear to you that I'm sayin' what I mean and mean what I say."

"Now, Li'l Man. Li'l Man, the Reverend is gonna be right mad when he hears you let this gal stand up in your own house and speak so disrespectful to your only sista. I'm family. Ma Dear raised you— I raised you—better'n that. If she was alive, she'd take a strop to you. Ain't this your house? Ain't them boys yours? I guess Junior really has become the man of this family. Is that how it is, Li'l Man? Junior runs this family now? Do I have to go get permission from him to be in this here house while this yellow heifer stands there mockin' me?"

Auntie had practically screamed this over Poppa, like left and right blows to his pride.

"Boys, now y'all get ya li'l asses in the room and put that suitcase away," says Poppa. "Ain't nobody leavin' this house tonight. I make the rules in this here house. I am still the man of this house and I says who come and who goes. This ain't Junior's house. This is my house. Now g'on back in that room and be still. Move!"

Poppa looks over at Auntie—it's much easier to do than looking at Momma.

My brothers start to walk back toward the room. Momma doesn't turn to look at them. She keeps her eyes fixed upon Poppa. She tells the boys not to move, to stand right where they are. And they do. For the first time, somethin' about Momma's voice tells them that Poppa's isn't the last word. Momma moves toward Poppa, and in her sway, I can tell the fight is no longer about just me.

" 'My wife, my boys, my house.' That's all you ever say. Well, this . . . this is my momma's house, J. T. She gave it to us—gave it to *me*. And I gladly shared it with you. But if it means that much to you, have it. I've cleaned it for you. You and your sister can sit here and have it. You can let her keep torturin' you if you like, but we are leavin'."

Momma turns and starts to walk toward the boys in the living room while Poppa gets up, throwing the chair out from under him, and starts after Momma.

As Poppa raises his hand, Junior appears at the screen door. All the boys run in front of Momma. Junior rushes in and grabs Poppa's hand.

"Junior! No! Junior, let him go!"

This was the first time during the conversation that Momma raises her voice. But right after, it found its way back down the scale to normal.

"It's okay, boys. Please, just go wait by the door. This is between your poppa and me," says Momma. The boys start to walk back to the door, all except Junior, who stands a bit in front of Momma.

"You're gonna hit me now, J. T.? Will that make you feel better? Feel like the man of the house? You gonna hit me in front of your boys? Is that what you want them to see? You've never hit me before, and now because of this woman, you think hittin' me will change somethin'?

"For hours, I've been thinkin' how I'd do it—how I'd leave. You know, I had a mind to just pack up and sneak out while you were gone. Is that how you want it? I could have killed Clariece in her sleep, and believe you me, I was mad enough to do it. But that's your fight, not mine. So, I said, *No, I'm better than that. I'm no possum in the street starin' down headlights, waitin' to be hit.* I waited here for you to come back. I wanted to tell you why I was leavin'. As your wife, I thought I owed you that. Because I love you, I owe you that. It was the right thing to do. Regardless of what anyone else does or thinks, I have to see that right still matters.

"There's nothin' I wouldn't do for you, even now. And that would be my choice, my pain, my sufferin', my joy. That, I gladly admit to, J. T. That's mine to do. But for me to ask my chilren to do the same isn't right. I'd rather raise chilren without a man than try raisin' a man and chilren, too. Yes, you're a good man, but I can't make you be. You'll have to do that for yourself. My work is done."

Poppa looks at each of the boys. He looks at Junior standing at Momma's side, ready for any move.

"S'pose you got somethin' to say, too, huh, Junior? You wanna tell me how I done you wrong, too?"

"Have you done me wrong, Poppa?"

"Listen here. Boy, you don't know—"

"I understand, Poppa. I understand," says Junior.

"Understand? You understand what, boy?!"

"I understand, Poppa. And it's awright. It's awright. I can understand now."

"It's awright." Those were the very words Poppa never got to say to his father. Hearing them now was like reliving a dream. He knew exactly what Junior meant, but at least Junior got to say it.

Poppa stands there with words lost. He looks at Junior, Junior at him. In their stare is an understanding, something that had not existed between them in the past. It had always been Poppa's understanding before, but today is different; it's as if they see each other—really look at each other—for the first time, free of any blame or resentment.

"I'll come back for more things later, when she leaves," says Momma. "You know where I'll be."

"Well, how touchin'. If this don't beat all," says Auntie. "Don't just stand there. Say somethin'. I come all the way here to do you a favor, raise a chile for you. You promised me this baby."

While Auntie is talking, I fall way low. I hear Leselle whisper, "Momma is peeing on herself." Junior tells Leselle what's going on and he starts crying. Momma just stands there like nothing is happening. There's no rush to clean this time. Finally, huddling the boys, she walks to the door. They began to walk out:

Junior.

". . . Li'l Man! Li'l Man, is you . . ."

Edward.

". . . goin' just stand there . . ."

Leon.

". . . and let that gal tell you off and . . ."

Leo.

". . . take my baby? That is my baby, Li'l Man! Now, you do somethin'. This is all your doin's . . ."

Momma.

"Li'l Man!"

Momma walks out through the screen door, catching it once again, refusing to let it slam, even now. She doesn't look back, just forward, as the moonlight casts its glow over her boys. As she walks down the steps, the boys come around by her side. The last thing heard coming from the house is Poppa crying, screaming, "My name is not Li'l Man! My name is Joseph—Joseph, Clariece! I'm not Li'l Man no more! You hear? No more!"

Momma stops and smiles at hearing Poppa saying

it, then her steps begin again. Any turning back that is to be done will have to be done by someone else this time. We walk around the house, toward the cornfield. Junior asks Momma if she'll be able to make it to Gram's house. She says she will. Leselle is still crying. The sky is empty, except for the full moon's watchful face hanging overhead. The moon looks as if it's following us, always right over our shoulders, yet leading the way.

We begin walking through the rows of corn, and before we are halfway, Momma tells Junior that I'm coming. As she eases down in between rows, Junior opens the suitcase and takes the clothes out, propping them under Momma's back. Blood stains her dress and Leselle begins to scream even more.

Momma once said that in Mississippi corn wasn't for nourishment, only to replenish the soil after it lost its fertility. And here she is in the cornfield about to give birth.

"It's okay; Momma. You're doin' fine." Then Junior screams to the boys, *"Go over there. All of you, go over there till I tell you. Leselle, stop cryin'!"*

Anna's breathing, breathing, breathing.

Then she stops.

There's a force behind it.

The breathing, breathing, breathing.

Force.

"Come on. Come on, Momma. The head is there. Leselle, be quiet!"

*"Junior, it's all right; let him scream," says Anna
on a held breath. "Let him scream."*

Breathing, breathing, breathing.

Then force.

*"The head is out, Momma. You're almost there,
just come on."*

Breathe. Breathe. Breathe.

"It's a girl, Momma. It's a girl," says Junior.

*Anna starts to cry as Junior hands the baby to
her.*

"A girl? A girl. Li'l Lisa. My li'l girl, Lisa Mae."

*The boys start coming closer, and the closer they
move to see the baby, the harder Anna cries. They
all kneel down around their mother and sister as if
the cornfield is as natural a place as any for them
to be. Anna keeps saying the baby's name and crying in between.*

*Leselle sits down next to them. He touches li'l
Lisa softly, then touches his momma.*

*"Momma. Momma, are you happy? Are you feel-
in' the Spirit?"*

"Yes, Leselle. Yes, I am."

Though the limbs of a tree may visibly shadow
the earth, below the surface is where the past
springs forth, making something simple into something intricate.

My mother recently mailed me a box filled with

dozens of letters. "Letters never sent." The letters were written while she was pregnant with me, including me in a space and time that sitting here, I can only deduce. Momma had told me numerous stories over the years, but these letters make me see that not only are women the bearers of life, we also provide the strength that makes life worth living. The note attached says:

My precious Lisa Mae:
We all have a huge desire for space. People so need it, though we tend to deny it. And a space does not necessarily mean length or width—a long space, a wide space, can appear small. No, the space we desire is the space above. We need that room overhead to remind us that there is something more, an aspiration.

In my old age, I'm beginning to sound more and more like your Gram Anderson. But no matter how old we get, the one lesson we must all learn is history is best served when addressed.

Remembering isn't always easy, especially when you'd rather forget. But certain things must end before others can begin.

Your Poppa sends his love.
Love, now and forever,
Mom

We all tend to want to jump to the end of the story, the last page, to see how it turns out. We have that desire to see that it's all going to work out, before we experience what it took to make it so.

The unknown is afloat within each of us. Some believe that if you speak, read, or play music to your unborn, it has an effect upon them. I can't rightly say I know, either way. But as I sit here, pregnant with my first child and going through these letters, I can't help but think of the life and the lives that preceded this one I now carry. Though a child may not know the why's and what-for's of a matter, we must believe that one need not know in order to sense, to feel.

What I didn't know until many years after my birth was that the sounds of my brother's tears were not the only ones coming from that cornfield. Poppa had left Auntie Clariece in the house screaming a name he no longer knew or answered to. As I was being brought into the world, he was several rows over, watching it all. I know this, because he told me. And as Momma would say, I was pleased to hear it.

I was conceived on a full moon and I was born on a full moon, but the view from here is much different, for I realize that even the faintest of lights begin in darkness. My eyes have been opened, my breath freed.